About the Author

Rachael Munro lives in Edinburgh with her husband and two children. She spent her childhood in Falkirk, the home of "The Kelpies", the largest equine sculpture in the world. Scotland is brimming with myths and legends that inspired her, growing up. She has had a passion for fantasy since her grandfather told his own fantastical stories to her, igniting her imagination.

Rachael is a Sunday school teacher, a classroom assistant and the mother of two daughters, spending most of her time around children, and behaving like one! She loves writing fantasy adventure fiction and her hobbies include painting, sculpting and other crafts.

Nymphas' World
Beyond the Onyx Mountains

R. C. Munro

Nymphas' World
Beyond the Onyx Mountains

Olympia Publishers
London

www.olympiapublishers.com
OLYMPIA PAPERBACK EDITION

A CIP catalogue record for this title is
available from the British Library.

ISBN: 978-1-80074-237-6

First Published in 2022

Olympia Publishers
Tallis House
2 Tallis Street
London
EC4Y 0AB

Printed in Great Britain

Dedication

I dedicate this book in affectionate memory of my grandma,
Catherine Haldane, for my life would not have been as
magical without her.

Acknowledgements

I first thank God for blessing me with the inspiration for this story and praise Him for His continuous wondrous ways. Thank you, Jesus, for your hand upon my life.

I secondly thank my husband, Alan, for supporting me every day with my writing ambitions and for giving me the courage not to give up.

I thirdly thank my father, Graham, mother, Gillian, father-in-law, John, and mother-in-law, Roberta, for all their encouraging words through the years and for making life magical.

I also thank my sister, Louise, and my brothers, Cameron and Euan, for reading and listening to my stories through the years and helping me to realise my potential.

I forever thank my church family, the Church of Hope in Edinburgh, for all their prayers and support through the hard years of my life.

I thank my best friends, Arlene and Hannah, for always being there for me and reading my stories.

I now thank Olympia Publishers for taking a chance on my story and bringing my dream to life.

Thank you, everyone!

-Chapter 1-
The Visitor at the Window

The night was quiet and still, with no clouds to spoil the bright, starry sky. A miniature boy of eleven appeared from behind a maple tree and watched the lights go out in the house before him. He smiled as he looked up at the house, and then flexed his insectile wings and buzzed over to a window, peering into where a girl lay sound asleep. Her long, curly red hair rested along her pillow and her lips curled into a smile as she dreamt.

Kay awoke and sat up quickly, shielding her eyes from the light that had intruded on her dreams, but all was dark and still. She got out of bed and went over to the window. Everything in the garden was in its proper place.

Her eyes felt heavy and she turned to go back to bed. Then, she saw a glimmer, reflecting in her mirror. Returning to the window, she saw a tiny golden light zooming around the flowerbeds.

Kay's heart leapt in her chest. She dived to the floor and snatched her slippers before creeping out into the hallway. She rushed down the staircase and out into the darkness, but saw no sign of the light. Kay waited in the garden, shivering in her pyjamas until, at last, there it was again — the floating light.

It looked like a bulb shining with golden dust and Kay leapt up to snatch it, but the light fled from her. She gave chase but tripped and crashed to the ground. She raised her head just in time to see the light fly out of the garden, ascending into the night sky.

Kay clambered to her feet, angry with herself for being so clumsy. She went back inside to her room and slid back into bed. She thought about the light until, eventually, she fell asleep.

*

The next morning, Kay arose sleepily from her bed and walked through to the living room, where her mother stood, ironing her school sweatshirt. Her mother was gazing out of the window, which looked out over her home town of Falkirk.

Belle Mackenzie glanced at her daughter, giving her a brief but pleasant smile. She was tall and slim with short, dark brown hair that curled softly around her pale face. Kay joined her mother at the window. Rows of bungalows were lined outside, each with identical terracotta-tiled roofs. Beyond Kay's street, was the rest of the town, descending into the valley. Giant pylons towered above the land and the British Petroleum Station sat to the right, spewing dark clouds into the atmosphere. The Ochil Hills finished the picture, sprawling across the countryside as far as the eye could see.

Belle handed Kay her sweatshirt, just as her brother Rob appeared in his pyjamas. Rob was eleven, a year older than Kay, and had dark brown hair, like his mother, with freckled cheeks and big ears, just like Kay. Rob had been Kay's closest friend but that was changing — Rob was now popular at school and Kay was not.

Kay returned to her room and slipped on her sweatshirt, disliking the royal blue colour that clashed with her red hair.

As she made her bed, she thought of the little light she had chased the night before; it made her feel happier than the thought of school and the lonely day it would bring.

"C'mon kids, school time! Kay, Rob, time to go!" called their mother.

Kay trundled obediently to the car.

Five minutes later, the car pulled up at the school and Kay sighed; the car journey was always too short for her liking. They got out of the car and kissed their mum goodbye.

"Rob, you'll never believe what I saw last night," Kay cried eagerly when they were alone.

"Maybe later, Kay," Rob told her as he spotted his friends and ran off to join them.

Kay was left alone and sat down under an old oak tree. All around her, kids were laughing, chattering and chasing each other. Kay longed to have a friend; someone to make her happy.

Kay pulled out her pencil and sketch pad. She drew happy faces, little stars, fairies... *That's it!* Kay thought, *the little light I saw last night was a fairy!*

"What are you doing, Weirdo?"

The voice startled Kay. She looked up at a pretty girl with straight, light brown hair and a sneer on her face. The girl was surrounded by friends, who all wore similar expressions. She laughed cruelly, and her friends laughed louder as they walked away from Kay. It was Margaret Harronton, the girl who thought she was better than everyone else. It was true that she was pretty, clever and popular, but Margaret wasn't a pleasant person. Margaret would make fun of her, whatever she did. She even told the other kids that people with red hair had a disease, so they stayed away from Kay.

The bell rang and Kay slowly walked over to the classroom door.

"Good morning, class," announced Mrs Rich as she pushed open the door and allowed the children to enter.

"Good morning, Mrs Rich," said the class, following one another inside.

Kay took her seat at the back left corner and looked out of the window as the register was called.

"Kevin Arthur…"

"Here," squeaked a boy from the front.

"Amy Beech…"

"And look at that horrible hairband she's wearing!"

Margaret's voice made Kay flinch.

"I heard she got her shoes from a dump yard!"

The comments continued as the teacher called the rest of the register.

"Has that girl even heard of a brush?"

"SHUT UP!" Kay roared suddenly, at the top of her lungs.

"I beg your pardon?" gasped Mrs Rich from the front of the classroom. "Go outside at once, young lady!" shouted the teacher.

Kay walked out of the classroom and slumped in the corridor, tears beginning to creep down her cheeks. After a while, the door opened and Kay scrambled to her feet, wiping her face with her sleeve. The teacher looked at her with sympathy.

"Kay, what's wrong?" she asked gently. "Why are you acting like this today?"

Kay felt tears roll down her face again.

"Everyone hates me."

"And why do they hate you?"

"Because I'm different from them."

"Well, there's nothing wrong with being different," Mrs Rich replied kindly. "It's the people who are different that make a difference in this world, Kay. Just you remember that."

She smiled and held out her hand to lead Kay back into the classroom. Kay took hold of the teacher's hand and walked quickly to her desk, looking at no one. She ignored Margaret's sniggers, as Mrs Rich's words had helped put her at ease.

Later that day, Mrs Rich decided to teach a spelling lesson.

"Kay, how do you spell 'friend'?"

Mrs Rich's voice interrupted Kay's thoughts.

"Em... F... R... E... N... D," she guessed.

"No, not quite," responded the teacher.

"Margaret, do you know the answer?"

Margaret sat up in her chair and smirked at Kay.

"Yes, Mrs Rich, F. R. *I*. E. N. D," she said politely.

"Correct," Mrs Rich said, turning back to her board.

Margaret then leant in Kay's direction and whispered cruelly, "Maybe if you had friends, you'd know how to spell it."

The rest of the day passed quickly, and Kay and Rob met their mother standing outside the school gates. As she ushered them to the car, she asked how their day had been. Rob shrugged.

"It was all right," he told her.

"What about you, Kay?" she enquired.

"Fine," Kay muttered as they drove off.

As soon as the car pulled up to the kerb, Kay and Rob jumped out, hung up their school gear, and went out to do their own thing. Rob went out with his friends, leaving Kay to her own devices. She searched her pockets, scavenging for loose change, and counted up nearly a pound in her palm. Kay went over to the shop and mulled over the juice, crisps and sweets on display, before deciding on a tube of Smarties.

"Hello, Kay. How's your mother doing, dear?" said the shopkeeper in her high-pitched voice.

"Just fine, Mrs Buchanan," Kay replied, putting her money in the shopkeeper's hand.

"Can I have a few of those boxes on the floor, please?" Kay asked with a mouthful of chocolate.

"Of course, dear, and please, call me Mary," replied the elderly woman cheerfully.

"Thank you, Mary," Kay chirped.

She skipped back to her house with the boxes under her arm, singing happily to herself. As she entered, she smelled her favourite meal — mince and tatties.

The Mackenzie family sat down for dinner and Kay scraped her plate until every last morsel had been consumed. She thanked her mother and went off into the garden.

Kay took the boxes Mrs Buchanan had given her, as well as a large ball of string from the kitchen. Carefully, she constructed a series of "box traps" and positioned them on the grass in the places where she'd seen the little light the night before. Underneath each box, Kay laid a couple of Smarties for the fairy.

After Kay had set her traps, she took a fairy book from her mother's bookshelf and returned to the garden to read. She opened the book and gazed at one of the pictures. There was a small, glowing woman with insect wings. She had long, blonde hair, flowing in the wind, and she wore a flowery dress as she danced amongst tall flowers. Turning her eyes from the page, Kay thought about what she had seen last night in the garden, then she looked up to see Rob wandering towards her.

"What *are* you doing?" asked Rob as his eyes followed the traps.

"I'm going to prove that I saw a fairy," Kay mumbled.

"Are you mad?" Rob called.

"No, I'm not! Stop saying I'm crazy and silly!" Kay shouted.

"I didn't, I only said you're mad; are you hearing things too?" Rob said, chuckling.

Kay growled and ran up the garden, but Rob ran after her.

"How are you going to prove it then?" he asked.

Kay turned to face her brother.

"I'll catch it, tonight. I'll get you up and show you it's there."

Rob stared at his sister through narrowed eyes.

"Fine, if you catch a fairy, you can wake me. But if it's not there, I'm telling Mum you're seeing things."

He stretched out his hand to seal the deal and Kay shook it in agreement as they grinned at one another.

*

Kay waited in her bedroom and watched outside for any sign of the little light. It was dark now, but she didn't switch her light on and the shadows from her furniture stretched creepily across the floor. Kay was tiring, so she lay on her bed. She'd run to the window at every glimmer of light. However, it was always passing cars and Kay eventually wandered back to her comfortable bed, closed her eyes and fell asleep.

Hours later, Kay opened her eyes and immediately saw

the light fleeting away from the window. She raced towards the window and saw it dancing amongst the flowerbeds and then beneath a trap. Kay gasped as it snapped down upon the little light... She had caught the fairy.

Kay ran through to her brother's room.

"Rob, Rob! Wake up! C'mon, the fairy's there," Kay whispered loudly into his ear.

Rob turned in his bed and grunted. He looked at his clock.

"Kay, it's three in the morning."

"Yeah, but you said I was to tell you if I saw the fairy and I have, so c'mon," Kay urged.

She shook him until he got up.

"Where is it?" Rob said, as he stretched and yawned.

"It's caught in my trap, I saw it," Kay told him.

Rob followed Kay out into the garden.

"You know, Mum will kill us if she finds out we're up at this time," Rob said.

"But this is amazing, Rob; I've caught a fairy!" Kay said breathlessly as she threw the box aside.

Under the box was the light, showering golden flecks. Kay leapt for it, but it was too fast and avoided her dive. She jumped to her feet and chased after it but missed with her second dive too. She glanced up to see Rob with his hands clasped tightly.

"I got it... I got it!" Rob cried.

"We need to put it in a jar or something," Kay said, examining Rob's entwined fingers.

"Kay, I can feel its feet, it really is a fairy, you were right," called Rob.

Kay gave a smile before running into the house. She could barely contain her excitement. She crept up the stairs and into the kitchen. She pulled out a jar of coffee from the cupboard, poured its contents away and ripped off the label. She ran out to the garden again with the jar open, at the ready.

"It's walking around my hands and keeps punching my fingers!" Rob said, as he put the fairy into the jar.

Kay quickly replaced the lid and they both peered in. Only a mist of sparkling dust could be seen, so they waited for the dust to settle and were surprised to find that the jar was empty.

"Where'd it go?" Rob said, snatching the jar from Kay and giving it a shake.

As he shook it, Kay could hear a faint tap on the glass, as though it still had something inside.

"Rob, wait!" Kay cried as her brother opened the jar.

Rob placed his eye over the rim and peeked inside, but he immediately gave a yelp and dropped the jar. The fairy's light flared into view, igniting the night sky before surging upwards and fading into the darkness.

"Rob, are you okay?" Kay asked her brother as he groaned, holding his eye.

"No, I'm not," he sobbed.

He moved his hand away to reveal swelling around his bloodshot eye.

"It punched me!"

Kay examined his eye and couldn't resist giving a little giggle.

"C'mon, let's get back inside," she said, gently guiding him back into the house.

They both crept up the stairs and into the kitchen, and Kay grabbed a bag of peas from the freezer to place on Rob's eye.

"We actually caught a fairy, Rob," Kay said cheerfully.

"Yeah, you were right, it must have been invisible in the

jar, and when I looked in, it attacked me."

Rob gave a grin, and Kay laughed.

"We can't tell anybody about this, I mean, no one will believe us anyway," Rob said as he examined his hands, speckled with golden dust. "You mean the way you didn't believe *me*?" Kay said.

"Yeah, well, I believe you now," he assured her, putting an arm around his sister and Kay smiled, hugging him back.

"I suppose we'll never see it again," Rob said.

"Well, it came back tonight. I think it likes our house," Kay said, beaming.

"We'd better get back to bed before Mum catches us in here," Rob suggested, and they both made their way back to their bedrooms.

Kay glanced at the old grandfather clock whilst passing through the hall; it was a quarter to four. Once she reached her bedroom, she heaved her duvet over herself and quickly fell fast asleep.

-Chapter 2-
The Picnic

Kay awoke the following day, shielding her eyes from the summer sun that was streaming through a gap in her curtains. It was Saturday and Kay had the luxury of a long lie-in in bed. When she rose, she went through to the kitchen and grabbed herself breakfast. Kay sat down at the table beside her mother, who was reading a newspaper.

"Morning," Kay said.

"Afternoon, actually," her mother corrected, grinning.

Rob came into the kitchen.

"What happened to *you*?" Belle gasped, as she spotted Rob's swollen eye.

She rushed over and examined his injury, but Rob struggled free from her grasp.

"It's nothing, Mum," he grunted, and then sat at the table.

Belle continued to fuss over Rob's eye, demanding to know what had happened.

"I just bumped it on a door," Rob told her, but Belle didn't look convinced.

Minutes later, Kay and Rob watched their mother leave the room and Rob quickly leant in towards Kay.

"What if we never see that fairy again and we're the only ones that know it exists?"

"So what if we are? At least we've *both* seen it," replied

Kay.

"Well, maybe we should tell someone." Rob suggested, but Kay shook her head.

"No, Rob! We can only ever tell someone if we catch it again. Nobody's going to believe us unless we can prove the fairy exists," Kay figured.

"But even if we *did* catch it again, it would just turn invisible," Rob argued.

"Yeah, I suppose, but I'm not going to be called mad again," she said as she left the table.

Kay decided that it would be nice to spend the day out in the garden. She found her old tartan picnic blanket and went downstairs, passing her mother on the way.

"Make sure you don't stand on any of my nice plants!" her mother warned, taking off her favourite gardening gloves.

"I won't, Mum," Kay replied with a smile.

Kay strolled up the garden and sat on her blanket beside a little red maple tree. She ran into the house to gather a mug of juice and a plate of tasty treats and brought them to her picnic spot. She ate whilst the sun pleasantly warmed her face.

Kay soon finished her treats and began making daisy chains, working busily until she saw a shimmer of light reflecting upon a plant pot. It reminded her of the fairy, and she decided that she must try and catch it again. *If I had a pet fairy, people would want to be my friend*, she thought. She sighed as she gazed at her half-formed daisy chain.

"I wish I had friends," she said softly, as a tear rolled down her cheek.

"I'll be your friend," responded a child's voice.

Kay jumped. The voice had come from behind her, so she spun around, but nobody was there.

"Hello, who's there?" Kay called out.

"Down here," whispered the voice.

Kay looked down and saw a small, fuzzy face gazing up at her from the grass; it was a daisy. Kay gave a scream that the whole street could have heard.

"No, don't scream, please, I just want to talk," the flower pleaded, and Kay fell silent with her mouth agape.

"How can you speak?" she asked.

"Please don't be frightened, I just want to be your friend," the flower said, innocently.

Kay watched the flower blink and move its eyes.

"Well," said Kay, before pausing to ponder what she could say to a flower. "What's it like being a daisy?"

"Why don't we talk about you," the daisy said, ignoring Kay's question. "What's your name?"

"My name's Kay," she told the flower as it beamed up at her.

"I'm Alva," it said, excitedly shaking its mane of white petals.

"So, Alva, why are you talking to me?"

"I think you're an interesting creature," Alva said.

Kay felt a little offended.

"'Creature'; I've never been called that before."

"Well, you've never spoken with a flower before, have you?" Alva said, proudly.

"I suppose," Kay answered.

She heard footsteps and turned to see Rob approaching.

"Hey, Kay, what's up?" he asked casually.

Kay turned back to the daisy, but it was motionless.

"Kay?"

"What!" she snapped.

"What's come over *you*?" Rob grumbled.

"Nothing," Kay sighed.

"Are you angry with me?" he asked, a little puzzled.

"No," Kay said glumly, as she looked back at the daisy.

"You're acting a bit strange," Rob said as he eyed the daisies too.

"I was just in the middle of something," Kay said awkwardly.

"What? A picnic by yourself... very important," Rob jested.

Kay frowned at him.

"C'mon, let's go inside, Mum says dinner's almost ready," Rob told her.

Kay picked the daisy, gathered her blanket and accompanied Rob into the house.

Rob wandered to the living room and threw himself onto the nearest armchair to watch television. Kay, however, went straight to her room and examined the daisy, but it showed no sign of life.

"Alva?" she whispered to the flower. "Hello, can you hear me?"

The flower did nothing. She shook it frantically to awaken it, but it still didn't speak.

"Say something!" Kay growled. "Please!"

The flower remained stubborn, and Kay became angry. She threw the flower across her room, and it landed by the window, losing its petals and breaking its stem.

"Oh, no!" Kay gasped. "I'm sorry, I didn't mean to hurt you," Kay pleaded. "Are we still friends?"

Kay stared at the limp flower, hoping that it would answer her, but there was nothing she could do for Alva now. *There's no wonder I have no friends*, Kay thought bitterly.

"Kay, I'm dishing up dinner now!" her mother yelled.

Kay sat down with the rest of her family, but she didn't feel hungry as she thought of the daisy.

Her mother let her leave the table and she went out to the garden, where she saw the boxes and suddenly remembered the fairy. Just then, Rob joined her in the garden.

"What are *you* up to?" he whispered with a grin.

"I'm resetting the traps," Kay replied.

"Oh, right, the fairy," Rob recalled.

"I hope it comes tonight, so we can catch it again," Kay said.

"You're totally obsessed with this fairy. Are you keen to get a black eye too?" Rob chuckled and Kay grinned with amusement.

"Who wouldn't try and catch a fairy if they could?" Kay questioned him.

"Someone who received a black eye from his last encounter with one," Rob told her with a smile. "C'mon, Mum wants us to go to the shop for her."

Kay and Rob walked over to the shop, but on their way back they spotted some unfriendly characters underneath the glow of the nearest lamp post. It was Margaret, with her friends, and her brother was close by too, with his friends.

"C'mon, let's get back to the house," Rob told Kay.

"Oh, look, it's that weirdo, Kay," Margaret called out and Kay looked pathetically down at her feet.

"Don't you call my sister a weirdo," Rob shouted back.

Margaret and her friends scowled.

"Don't tell me what to do, Gorilla Face, or you can answer to my brother," screeched Margaret, loud enough for her brother to hear.

Rob glanced over to the group of boys and a large figure stepped forward. He had short, light brown hair and threatening eyes under his dark eyebrows.

"Let's go, Kay," Rob said, sounding worried.

They dashed towards their house, but Rob was grabbed by the larger boy.

"Don't you talk to my sister again, Mackenzie, or you'll answer to me," he snarled.

"Get off me," Rob growled, struggling against the boy's grip.

The boy looked mad and motioned to hit Rob but stopped as he heard a voice coming from the Mackenzie house.

"What's going on?" Belle cried loudly. "Get away from my children!"

The boy quickly released Rob and they all ran off down the street, hollering insults. Rob and Kay approached their mother, Rob a bit shaken.

"What was that all about?" she asked, with grave concern.

"Just an idiot who thinks he can threaten me," Rob replied, angrily.

Kay was still in shock. She had not even attempted to help her brother; all she had done was watch on, feebly.

"Get inside," their mother said, with an exasperated voice, and Kay and Rob ran into the house.

Kay went through to Rob's room and found him sitting on his bed, looking glum.

"Are you okay?" Kay asked, softly, placing a hand on her brother's back.

"Yeah, I'm all right," Rob replied in a sullen voice.

"I've still to set the traps," Kay said, enthusiastically.

"Want to help me?"

Rob nodded and followed Kay outside, and the pair worked hard to reset the traps.

"There, that'll catch it," Rob announced, evidently pleased with himself.

Kay and Rob went to bed and waited for midnight to arrive. They slipped out of their beds and made their way to the garden. No traps had fallen; Rob and Kay glanced at one another with disappointment.

They waited in the garden for hours, but nothing came. They tried all week but eventually gave up. Kay felt saddened that the fairy might never return.

The next morning was the last day of term and Belle told Kay and Rob that she couldn't drive them home from school because she was working later.

When Kay and Rob entered the playground, they spotted Margaret's brother, Boris, more commonly known as Harron. Kay knew that Rob had been trying to avoid Harron since their encounter in the street, but this was hard when they were in the same class. Kay had asked Rob why Harron bothered him. He figured that Harron was jealous that Rob was so easy liked, whilst Harron lived by his hard reputation. Kay wished that she was big and strong, then she would be able to thump Margaret and Harron whenever they picked on them. She hated them both.

Kay felt happy that another miserable school year had ended. All that was left to be faced was Mrs Rich's 'fun work'. The excited children entered the classroom boisterously and Mrs Rich stood at the front.

"Right, class, divide yourselves into six groups of five," she said, counting the bobbing heads. "We're doing a quiz today."

The class rushed to move their desks beside their friends. Kay was far less excited about this. She hesitated as she scanned the classroom. The teacher raised her head to find Kay standing alone by her desk.

"All right, Kay, you can join Ian's group," Mrs Rich told her, gesturing towards the remaining team with just four pupils.

Kay shuffled timidly across the room and laid her desk next to a boy with a runny nose. He glared at her unpleasantly, whilst wiping his snot on his sleeve. Ian had curly, dark brown hair and his cheeks were two clusters of freckles. Kay looked away from Ian and glanced at another boy, who was chewing the end of his pencil. This boy's name was Stephen. He had a long face, buck teeth and big ears. Kay thought he had a strong resemblance to Bugs Bunny as he chewed his pencil. The other members of Kay's group were a short, brown-haired girl called April and a blonde, spotty boy called Craig.

The quiz continued throughout the early morning, and her team did poorly. At half past ten, she and her class went out for break. They were all loud and excited that the school year had almost ended.

Kay anxiously trailed behind and walked over to the old oak tree. She scanned the playground from the safety of the shadows and saw Harron again, with his friends, harassing a young boy. She also caught sight of Rob, standing as far away from Harron as possible, looking nervously over his shoulder.

As Harron moved around the school grounds, Rob moved in the other direction, without him noticing. Kay brought out her drawing pad to hide behind and, peeking over the top, watched as Harron stomped by her. Kay gave a sigh of relief.

The bell rang and Kay made her way into class, where arts and crafts materials were laid on each desk. This was Kay's favourite activity, because she was good at art. All around her desk lay a variety of materials, in many different colours and shades.

"I want you all to make your parents an end-of-term present," Mrs Rich called out.

Kay immediately grabbed some yellow card and a glitter pen, knowing exactly what she was going to create — the fairy. She drew the outline of the fairy and glued a bright yellow pom-pom for its head. She shaped its limbs with layers of craft foam, which were then covered in light green felt for its little dress. Light blue tissue paper was carefully crafted into a set of wings, while its features were created with glitter.

Kay applied the finishing touches to her fairy and then sat back, allowing her thoughts to wander into a daydream. She rested her head in her arms and thought of the fairy. Kay jumped as a pom-pom packet fell on her.

"Oh, sorry," said Ian, as he rescued the remaining pom-poms from falling on Kay.

"That's okay," said Kay shyly.

Ian gave a smile and then walked over to Mrs Rich, to show her his completed work. It seemed that everyone had almost finished their crafts, so Kay placed her fairy with the other pieces, eager to collect it again at home time.

Kay saw that everyone was with their friends, admiring one another's creations, so she sullenly returned to her desk and sat alone, staring out the window. Mrs Rich left the room to check on another class. It was then that Kay heard a faint sound and saw a pencil rolling slowly across her desk. It stopped on top of a sheet of card and then lifted from the desk, hovering in front of her. Kay gasped.

-Chapter 3-
The Chip Shop

The pencil swooped down to the surface of the card and started to write in long and flowing motions.

Hi. It's Alva.

Kay gasped and grabbed her own pencil to reply.

Where are you?

The pencil came to life again.

I'm outside.

Whereabouts outside?

Somewhere no one can see me, it replied.

Why? Kay questioned.

There was no response. Kay glowered at the stubborn pencil.

Why are you talking to me?

I want to be your friend. You seem lonely.

Kay smiled, feeling happy, in a way. Although she couldn't see Alva, she still had someone to talk to.

Alva, what are you?

At that moment, the pencil dropped and bounced across Kay's desk.

"And what is *this* supposed to be?" called the familiar, irritating voice of Margaret.

Kay peered around to see Margaret waving her fairy around to gain attention. Margaret snatched the tissue paper wings from the card and threw them to the floor in a crumpled heap.

"No!" screamed Kay, running towards Margaret.

"You should've glued it properly, it's rubbish!" she said with a sneer. Margaret tossed the fairy aside and triumphantly returned to her desk, laughing along with her friends. Kay felt so angry that she thought she might hit her.

Mrs Rich returned and announced, "Right, class, it's almost bell time. I want you all to stand behind your seats and we'll see who knows their times tables."

Mrs Rich quizzed the children, and a queue began to form at the door with every correct answer. It took Kay a few attempts to answer a question correctly but eventually she snatched up her fairy and its wings and stood at the end of the rather large line of pupils. Margaret's friends, Rebecca and Mandy, were last to join the queue.

When the bell finally sounded, the children sprinted into the distance, leaving screams of joy echoing behind them. Once Kay got outside, she waited for Rob beside her favourite oak tree, and watched Harron march out of the school with some other large boys. Rob soon followed and strolled over to meet Kay.

"Hey, Rob, glad school's over?" Kay asked with a grin.

"Yup," Rob replied and then he frowned, noticing Harron's group disappear around the corner. "I think we should walk the other way," he said nervously.

"Okay," Kay agreed, and they set off down into the valley of streets leading them the long way home.

However, this proved to be a bad idea when Kay and Rob encountered Margaret and her friends.

"Let's walk on the other side of the road," Rob suggested,

guiding Kay off the kerb, but Margaret followed.

"I can't believe you don't know your times tables!" giggled Margaret, as she strode across the road after them.

"Shut your trap," Rob snapped.

"I mean, do you know anything or are you really that stupid?"

Kay could hear Rob's defensive comments, but they barely registered as hatred built up inside her. Margaret's friends were laughing and their remarks echoed in Kay's head. Before she knew it, she had confronted Margaret.

"Well, I'm better than Mandy; she was last out the class!" Kay shouted.

Silence fell upon the street and Margaret was suddenly angry too.

"Are you making fun of one of my friends?" Margaret snarled, stooping into Kay's face.

"You're the one who's making fun of *her!*" Rob shouted back at Margaret.

"Shut up, my brother will take care of you... very soon!" Margaret spat back, as her friends gathered around Kay, pushing Rob out of the way.

"*Are* you calling Mandy stupid?" said Margaret sharply, screwing her eyes at Kay.

"No, she's just as good as me at tables," said Kay in frustration.

Margaret pushed Kay and she dropped her fairy on the ground.

"You're the one that's so stupid you don't have any friends, you loser!"

Margaret stomped Kay's fairy into the ground and all the girls started to chant "Loser" with malicious pleasure.

Kay pushed Margaret back, screaming, "I do have friends!" All the girls changed their chant to "Fight" and pushed Kay towards Margaret.

Margaret lunged at Kay, but suddenly a blast knocked them both backwards.

Kay fell to the ground but sat up just in time to see blue electrical sparks fizz between her and Margaret. Some of the girls ran away screaming when they saw Margaret lying flat on her back.

Rob crashed down beside Kay. "Kay, are you all right?"

"Yeah, I think so," she responded, looking around her in a daze. "What happened?"

"I think you two were hit by lightning or something," Rob told her, looking scared.

"You're a freak," Margaret screamed, pointing at Kay. "She cursed me with black magic," she continued, staggering as she got up.

Kay rose to her feet and Margaret took a few steps backwards, along with her friends. They all ran off, shrieking "Witch" and "Freak".

Kay and Rob continued homeward, but Kay was still shaken by what had happened. Rob could see his sister tremble and turned around every so often to ask, "Are you okay?"

Rob and Kay approached their street and Rob put his arm around Kay as they entered their house. Her mind was a haze as she climbed the stairs and shuffled into the living room. Rob hugged her tenderly, and tears trickled from Kay's eyes. She didn't know what had happened between her and Margaret, but she began to wonder whether she was a *freak*.

The day's events flashed through her mind and Kay remembered the floating pencil.

"Rob," Kay said. "In school, there was this pencil... "

"Right," Rob said, breaking their embrace.

"It started moving and writing by itself. It told me that it wanted to be my friend, and the other day a flower started talking to me as well, but it's the same person."

"A person," Rob said, surprised. "You think things are talking to you now? Kay that's craaa... "

He glanced at Kay's delicate expression and coughed loudly to disguise what he had been about to say.

"Look, Rob, remember the fairy out in the garden? Remember how you didn't believe me then?" Kay looked straight into her brother's eyes, thinking it would convince him if she didn't blink.

"Does Margaret bother you often?" Rob asked, changing the subject.

"Yes," Kay croaked.

"Well, that's school over now. Mum won't be able to do anything until after the summer holidays," Rob said, but Kay had already walked away to hide in her room.

She shut the door, curled up on her bed and wept.

Later on, Kay's mother came home from work and Rob told her about what had happened. Belle opened Kay's bedroom door, and seeing the look on her daughter's face, rushed straight over to give her a comforting hug.

"What happened?" she said, tenderly stroking Kay's hair.

Kay gushed about how she was picked on by Margaret every day and that she always said she was strange or stupid.

"You're not stupid or strange," Belle whispered, with a soothing tone.

"But I am, Mum, I don't even have any friends," Kay retorted, with a tear rolling off the end of her chin.

"*I'm* your friend," her mother said softly.

Kay gave her a smile.

"It doesn't matter what others think, you're special to me. You're my daughter and I'll always love you."

Belle was tearful as well and they talked the whole evening. Kay felt much better knowing she would always have a friend in her.

The next morning, Kay was a great deal happier. It was the first day of the summer holidays and she had planned an outing in the town with her mother. They both traipsed around the many shops as Kay tried to find clothes to her liking. Unfortunately, she was exceptionally difficult when it came to clothes; they had to be exactly to her taste.

"What about this one, Kay? It looks so pretty," Belle said, showing her a light pink top decorated with purple and blue butterflies.

"No, I like *this* one better," Kay told her, pulling out a t-shirt with an interesting glowing spider across it.

Her mother frowned, but when she saw Kay's expression, she smiled at her.

"If you're sure," she said, handing Kay the money.

Kay had lunch with her mother and then they both went home. Kay could barely move from the amount she'd eaten, so she slumped on her bed and watched a DVD.

Most of Kay's DVDs were Disney movies; a film with a "happily ever after" made her feel good. She picked out *Mulan*. Kay greatly enjoyed this movie, because she liked how tough Mulan was and also the idea that there were spirits to guide her. Kay didn't know what to believe about spirits, but she wanted them to be real. Whenever she thought of spirits, she thought of her father.

Kay was only two years old when her father died whilst serving in the army. She liked to think that her father was with her, so she had someone to talk with when she needed to most.

"Dad," Kay said, "please help Mum find someone; someone who will make her happy and stop crying..." Kay trailed off as Rob entered.

"Who are you talking to?" Rob asked, scanning the room.

"Knock!" screamed Kay, irritated that he had caught her talking to apparently nobody.

"Look, Kay, I believe you about the talking flowers and pencils and stuff. I mean, all these things can't be happening coincidentally," he said, wandering around the room.

"What are you saying?" Kay said, switching off her television.

"Well, the fairy and the lightning were quite magical, so you must be a sorcerer," he concluded.

"What!" Kay exclaimed. "I'd know if I were magic or not, Rob."

"Some sorcerers take a while to tap into their powers," he rambled and Kay rolled her eyes.

"I'm not the one doing the magic, it's someone called Alva."

"Let's try and talk to this "Alva" then," Rob said encouragingly, and he took her hand and led her outside.

They both sat in amongst the daisies, talking to them. Kay thought that they must have looked crazy, talking to the flowers. The daylight was now dimming.

"It's not working," said Rob, looking agitated and bored.

Kay heaved a sigh, feeling that the day had been wasted.

Kay and Rob went in for their dinner, but they barely ate a thing, leaving the table almost as hungry as when they arrived.

Kay went back to her room and watched more of *Mulan*, before Rob burst into her room wearing his blue jacket.

"Knock," Kay moaned.

"Sorry," Rob said, "do you want to come with me to the chippy to get some chips? Mum says we can."

"Sure," Kay replied, smiling.

Kay and Rob journeyed down their long street, passed under the bridge that took them safely beyond the roundabout and then along a smaller street to the chip shop. They ordered their dinner and strolled over to the wall outside the shop where they ate their steaming chips, savouring every bite. They watched the sun sink below Callendar Park Woods, whilst licking their sticky fingers.

They walked up the steep hill to the mouth of their street in silence. Kay noticed that Rob was still eating his chips.

"Yuck, aren't they cold?" Kay said, screwing her face up.

"Yeah, but they still taste good," he said, stuffing a few more into his mouth.

Kay rolled her eyes at him and grinned.

"What, I'm savouring the salt. Mum never cooks with…"

Rob broke off and stopped where he was. Kay followed his gaze and saw silhouettes emerging over the hill.

"It's Harron!" he warned her, with a tremulous voice.

Rob stuffed his paper chip bag into his pocket and turned, looking over his shoulder to see if Harron had seen them. Unfortunately, he had.

Rob and Kay walked briskly back towards the chip shop, hearing the thunder of Harron and his gang's footsteps behind them. Kay and Rob darted up to the high school, but they were easily catching up with them. Rob dashed across the road, leaving Kay on the pavement.

"No, Rob!" Kay shouted, as he was almost hit by a car.

"C'mon, Kay!" Rob screamed from the other side.

Harron ran towards Kay and she leapt off the pavement, her heart hammering in her chest. She heard the beeping of horns from cars hurtling towards her, blinding her with their lights. Rob pulled Kay off the road and the pair started climbing up a grassy hill to Callendar Park Woods. They ran across a large open field that led to surrounding trees, Rob almost dragging Kay as he grasped her hand tightly.

They reached the trees, clutching at them for support as they gasped for breath. In the distance there were sounds of cars screeching and skidding, their horns beeping, and they knew that Harron had crossed the road.

Rob was static, listening intently as the traffic returned to its usual sounds and pace. The sun had now completely vanished below the horizon and only a scattering of rays illuminated the area around them. Kay's eyes began to adjust, allowing her to see Harron and his gang rising up over the hill.

-Chapter 4-
The Rowan Tree

Rob snatched Kay's hand and they weaved through the trees to escape. Kay felt branches scratch her face and neck, but she couldn't stop or slow down, for fear of Harron.

Rob bent down and crawled into the midst of the bushes and Kay followed, receiving more scratches on her face. She glanced nervously at her brother, breathing as quietly as she could and listening. Soon enough, they heard the voices of Harron and his gang approaching.

"They went this way; look, footprints," said one of the gang.

"Don't be stupid, that could be anyone's footprints," said another.

"Shut up, the both of you," Harron shouted, "look what *I* found."

Rob gasped when he saw Harron holding his paper chip bag.

"They're here!" Harron grinned and his gang started to shake the bushes, uncovering Rob and Kay immediately.

Rob was grabbed, but Kay managed to squeeze out of the bushes, evading their clutches.

"Run, Kay… run for it!" Rob bellowed and Kay sprinted into the woods.

She realised she was being tailed, so she ducked under

low branches to slow her pursuer. Soon the boy was far behind her and Kay hid again.

Kay peered around for the boy who had chased her but he wasn't anywhere in sight, so she proceeded to go back for Rob. As Kay got closer, she could hear Harron shouting. She peeked over the nearest bush to see her brother curled up on the ground, with Harron kicking him. Kay felt a surge of anger but was seized by a strong pair of hands and hauled out of the bushes in front of Harron. Rob sprang up when he saw Kay, wincing as he held his stomach.

"Hold her; I'll deal with *her* in a minute," Harron snarled.

Kay knew this would end badly, so she stamped on the foot of the boy who was holding her and he let go, crying out in pain. She lunged for Harron, landing on his back before he could hurt Rob any more. There was a sudden burst of blue electric light and Kay shot backwards into a tree. Her eyes burned, blinded by the flash. She felt a hand pull her up and her eyes refocused to see it was Rob.

Blue light was illuminating their surroundings and Kay saw a giant electrical bubble caging Harron and his gang. Harron looked just as scared as Margaret had and Kay felt rather scared too.

"Did *you* do that?" said Rob, with a mixture of fear and awe.

"No!" squeaked Kay, who was still quite traumatised.

"Let's get out of here," Rob said, pulling Kay back into the trees.

They had only taken a few steps when someone spoke.

"Are you two, okay?"

"Who's there?" Rob called.

"It's Alva!" squeaked the voice, coming from the trees.

"Show yourself!" Rob yelled, his voice shaking.

There was a sudden glow in the darkness that drifted out from behind a tree in front of them. It was gold in colour and as it got closer, Kay realised it was the fairy.

"Stay back!" Rob shouted, thinking of his last encounter with the fairy.

"So, it was you!" Kay cried, finding her voice. "You were the flower and the pencil and *you* did this." She pointed towards Harron.

"Yeah, it was me, "Alva said. "I hope I didn't hurt you, I've not quite got used to that spell yet."

The fairy came to rest on a leaf, keeping its distance.

"You're not going to trap me again, are you?" asked the fairy, its light of swirling dust dimming as it spoke.

"No, I'm sorry about that," Kay apologised, rather embarrassed.

"Wait, Kay, don't talk to it," Rob warned her. "It could blow us into the next world!"

"Oh, no, I don't think I could do that, but I could try," Alva said, rising up into the air again.

"No!" shouted Rob and Kay at the same time.

"Don't worry, I was only joking," Alva laughed.

The fairy dimmed its glow further to reveal a two-inch young boy with bug wings. He smiled at them and Kay didn't feel afraid at all.

All of a sudden, the woods grew darker and the sounds of voices and snapping twigs were heard nearby. Harron and his friends were not in the bubble any more.

"I forgot," squeaked Alva, "the Bubblo spell doesn't hold that long, unless you're a really powerful Nympha."

"You mean they've escaped?" Rob shouted, as he and Kay

began to run.

"Follow me," the fairy chirped with excitement, zooming into the darkness of the woods.

Kay and Rob leaped over fallen trunks and branches as they pursued Alva, the trees echoing the calling of Harron's gang closing in.

"Why are we following it?" Rob cried anxiously.

"He'll lead us to safety!" Kay shouted back.

"But where are we going, what about Mum?" Rob asked.

"I don't know where we're going, but we need to get away from Harron," Kay called back.

"But how can we trust a fairy?" Rob argued.

"I trust him, he's my friend," Kay decided.

"What?" Rob called out in disbelief.

The fairy kept on going, deeper and deeper into the woods, until the voices of Harron and his gang faded.

"Where are you taking us?" Rob demanded.

"To Nymphas' World," Alva responded enthusiastically.

Kay gave a shriek as something touched her hand. It was the fairy's tiny little hand, that couldn't even fit over the width of one finger. Alva began to tug at Kay's finger to guide them in the right direction.

"Where on Earth is that?" called Rob, grabbing onto Kay as the fairy led the way.

"It's not on Earth," the fairy called back.

"What? You mean you live in space?" exclaimed Rob sceptically.

"No, I live through the tree roots and beyond the Portal," Alva responded.

"You must be joking!" Rob shouted at a volume the whole forest could hear.

"How much farther is it?" Kay asked, feeling cold and tired.

"It's just another eighteen trees down!" the fairy called back.

Eventually they reached a moonlit clearing that Kay and Rob didn't recognise.

"Isn't it beautiful?" the fairy exclaimed, pointing to the earthy, bare patch of ground.

"What is?" said Rob, staring all around at the circle of trees.

"The tree; isn't it magnificent!" Alva declared. Kay and Rob turned around on the spot trying to see what Alva was gazing at.

"There are a lot of trees here," Kay said, feeling confused.

"Oh, I forgot you two can't see it!" the fairy squeaked with a chuckle.

Alva buzzed right up to Kay's face and sprinkled a glittery substance that drifted gently through the air towards her.

"Keep your eyes open and you'll see the tree," the squeaky voice said, as the substance softly formed over her eyes, glazing them gold.

The fairy flew over to Rob and repeated what he had done to Kay. He then pulled back to show them what they hadn't seen before.

There, where the bare earth had been, stood a tree with petite, bright green leaves and a multitude of little red berries, bunched tightly together on the branches. The bark was rough and worn, bearing the scars of age in deep grooves. It had a golden magical glow to it, reminding Kay of Christmas; the berries like tiny red glass baubles. Kay and Rob stepped closer, examining the small hole in the trunk: it wasn't dark inside the hole but shone an electric blue, just like the fairy's bubble.

"It is beautiful," Kay said, admiring the tree.

"This is the Rowan Tree," Alva announced. "It's the way to Nymphas' World."

"And how exactly do we get there?" said Kay, frowning.

"Through here," squeaked Alva, pointing into the hole.

"We won't fit in there," Rob said, shaking his head at the little fairy.

Alva grinned and touched the tree. Magic dust began pouring onto the bark and swirling around the tree's entire structure. Gradually, the Rowan grew to an enormous height until it was larger than all the trees around it. The bark surrounding the hole rolled inside the tree, expanding the gap into an archway that was big enough for Kay and Rob to fit through. Kay felt a little afraid as she peered into the entrance of the tree. It still had a blue glow, but she could not see anything below.

In the distance came the sound of voices, which startled them all.

"C'mon, we've got to hurry!" cried Alva as he flew down into the tunnel.

Kay and Rob were quick to follow.

Kay screamed as she plunged deep into the void. Eventually, she landed on a bark-textured floor and Rob soon fell down beside her. Alva was flying above them and seemed larger than before.

"Where are we?" Rob asked, rubbing his sore bottom.

"We're inside the tree roots," Alva said. "Sorry about the hard landing; it's meant for Nymphas, because we can fly down."

Kay and Rob both groaned.

"This way," Alva called, urging them to get up.

Kay and Rob stumbled down a long, bumpy corridor, with protruding roots that caught their feet. There seemed to be many corridors of roots leading all over, each dimly lit with glowing spheres floating in mid-air. As they delved farther into the depths it felt like they were back in the forest again. Kay was scared but excited at the same time. She looked up at Alva's wings whirring in front of her and noticed he was getting bigger and was now half the size of Kay.

"Hey, you're bigger!" Rob exclaimed from behind Kay, noticing the change too.

Alva stopped flying and floated to the ground, his head reaching the top of Kay's legs.

"Yeah, I thought it was weird being small too," he said.

"That's not what I meant," Rob muttered to himself, giving Alva a funny look.

"Almost there!" Alva called as he walked down the tunnel.

Kay and Rob could now see the shine of the electric blue light again as they weaved through the winding corridors. The space in the root became tighter, and soon they were crawling, before squeezing through what seemed to be the end of the root.

They emerged into a hollow cavern and Kay and Rob gasped. There before them was a swirling circular wall of magnificent liquid, floating unaided like a slowly moving whirlpool. The colours were amazing, mingling in seductive spirals that drew Kay and Rob's eyes to the yellow spark in the middle of this strange flowing pool.

"Wow, what is it?" Rob asked in wonder.

"It's a portal; *the* Portal, actually," Alva answered as he let

Kay and Rob absorb what they were seeing.

Kay moved forward, transfixed by the Portal. She was afraid and anxious about what lay beyond it, but felt compelled to move closer by its hypnotic movement. She dipped her finger into the liquid and shuddered as a cool sensation washed over her skin. She hesitated a moment but then thrust her whole hand into the Portal. She suddenly recoiled as a rough wind chilled her fingers. Kay panicked; it was all too strange for her.

"It's only a portal, it takes you to Nymphas' World," Alva said encouragingly, waiting for them to go through.

Rob wandered over to Kay and gave her a weak smile. He then grasped her hand and they both took their first steps into a new world.

-Chapter 5-
Edenland

Kay and Rob were caught in a silent, misty hurricane that drove them forwards. Rob led the way and Kay gripped tightly to his hand. Rob walked with his free hand outstretched, searching for an opening. His hand then suddenly shone golden as he found the way out and soon his whole body was passing through. Kay followed and they both stepped out of the Portal.

Kay and Rob opened their eyes. They were surrounded by tall and very old trees, which looked like they had been growing since the beginning of time. Above the treetops Kay and Rob could see a dark, purple sky with only three stars, each sparkling like large diamonds, in a triangular formation. On the ground, giant toadstools dotted the landscape as far as the eye could see.

Kay stood silently, thinking she could hear whispers coming from the trees. Calm had settled upon her, like the mist that lay at her feet, lingering above the earthy ground. Lines of black egg-shaped plants created a path that led into the shadows ahead. Kay followed the path until she saw a spectacular sight.

The ground descended into a valley below, bathed in the light of two moons: one white and one red. An enormous tree loomed at the left side of the valley and two gigantic bushes reached out above a dense forest. At the foot of the enormous tree, luminous balls were arranged in rows, streaming into an immense field. Farther away, Kay could see a wild swamp, leading up to a range of dark mountains, standing ominously on the horizon.

Now and then, Kay and Rob heard peculiar animal calls and were a little startled when they heard an unfamiliar voice behind them.

"Hi, are you okay?" asked the childlike voice.

Kay and Rob spun around to find Alva standing before them, just as big as themselves. His voice wasn't squeaky any more.

"Yeah, we're okay," Kay answered, whilst Rob gawked at him.

Alva had short, bright yellow hair and pointy ears. His eyes were much more luminous than that of a human, glittering like blue crystals, and his skin glowed golden. He walked over to Kay and Rob, studying them curiously. Kay looked at him with equally keen interest. She looked at his hands and saw that they were just as big as her own but had no fingers; instead, he had thumbs at either end of his hands. His wrists had golden patches that sparkled with dust.

The fairy wore garments that were leaf-like in shape and design, covering his shoulders and torso and draping down to his knees. Kay glanced at his feet as well; he had two big toes on each foot that took up the space of a human's five toes.

"C'mon, I'll hide you until it's safe for you to go home."

Alva led the way and Kay saw his beautiful wings properly for the first time. They were translucent with golden veins stretching across them. He also had under-wings that appeared when he flicked his top wings. The wings were that of a damselfly and folded against his back.

"This is Elna Wood, and we're in Edenland in Nymphas' World," Alva explained. He looked up to the sky. "Those three stars up there change the weather. My mum thinks that's where the Mother of All, stays."

"Who's she?" Rob asked.

"She is the one that made all Nymphas and brought peace to Edenland."

Alva stopped talking as he heard a rustle in the bushes up ahead. A bird hopped out, cawing like a crow. It had dark green plumage and four legs. Alva gave a sigh of relief.

"Good, only a Chuckle... for a moment there I thought it might be something dangerous. You see, Humans aren't really supposed to be here. In fact, you're probably the first Humans to enter Nymphas' World for hundreds of years."

"You mean we might get in trouble for being here?" Rob asked.

"Yeah, especially if the Onyx find you; as far as they're concerned, it's illegal for you to be here," Alva said. "The Onyx hate Humans, so it's best to stay hidden."

"Who, are the Onyx?" Kay asked

"They're a very dangerous race of Nympha," Alva replied, "so we have to be careful."

Alva led Kay and Rob farther into the woods. The surrounding trees were starting to thin and Kay could see something moving between them that she thought looked like a giant.

"Alva, what's that up ahead?" Kay asked anxiously, stopping them all from going any farther.

Alva smiled.

"That's the Great Statues," he laughed, running towards

them.

Kay and Rob ran along too, trusting there was nothing to fear.

The giant statues were in a clearing and stood taller than the tops of the old trees. They were bronze-looking, but the most bizarre thing about them was that they could move. The first statue was a woman; she bore no wings and had garments that floated behind her. She was old and wise-looking, with stringy hair waving like her clothes. She smiled constantly, always looking at them and turned her head as they moved on.

"That's Gaeatra Lush, more commonly known as, the Mother of All. Like I said, she was the oldest living Nympha that created the first of our kind," Alva told them.

"She looks human; why does she have no wings?" Kay asked curiously.

"She did have wings, but everyone argues about what kind she had, so the statue has none," Alva explained. "She travelled all of Nymphas' World, documenting every spell known today. She was very old when she died."

There were six statues all together of historical Nympha figures, from warriors to kings. The last statue was an old male fairy with one damaged wing. His name was King Edwin Clover, and Alva told Kay and Rob that he was the present king of the Ever Nymphas.

"What's an Ever Nympha?" Kay asked as she looked at the last statue.

"*I'm* an Ever Nympha!" Alva chuckled. "There are four races of Nympha: Ever, Floatly, Feature... and Onyx," he said, scowling at the last word.

Alva led the way out of the trees and Kay and Rob found

themselves facing hundreds of giant foxglove flowers, each surrounded by massive green bubbles. Kay ran up to one of them to touch it but Alva grabbed her fingers before she could.

"Don't touch them," he said sternly. "You must know the password before you can enter."

Kay felt her cheeks go red; she had to be more careful.

"Look!" Rob shouted out as an exotic bird flew down towards one of the green bubbles.

The bird was light blue with a large beak and streaming green tail that it struggled to carry. The moment the creature landed on one of the bubbles it bounced back off again, springing high into the air and out of sight. Kay and Rob looked at Alva.

"This is my village and those are the Ever Nymphas' houses."

All the flower houses were in single file, and each bubble had a path of brightly coloured rainbow stones leading down to dividing roads. Kay thought the village looked cheerful.

"I want us to go around the village, so no one spots you. C'mon, this way!" Alva called out, flying around the village.

Alva took Rob and Kay into another wooded area and Kay could see eyes, noses and smiles upon the tree trunks. She heard the short hoots and sharp cries of strange animals again as they walked deeper into the woods. Rob jumped any time he heard something unusual and one noise sent him into panic; it sounded like an owl's hoot but it ended with a parrot's screech.

"What was that?" Rob cried, backing away from the noise.

"That was a Bubow," Alva replied, "they're harmless."

"Where are we going?" Kay asked, keeping close behind

Alva.

Alva grinned as he ducked under a branch and called on them to follow. Kay and Rob ducked under the branch and raised their heads to find an enormous waterfall surrounded by lush green plants. The water was clear and sparkling under the double moons' glow; flecks of water danced around the bottom, accompanied by a frothy mist, appearing mystical and mysterious. Around the banks of the falls were blue, purple and pink flowers; Kay thought this was like something she had dreamed of, through many fairy tales, but this wasn't a dream and now she was *in* a fairy tale.

Alva flew over to the base of the falls.

"This is my den," Alva told Kay and Rob as they wandered up beside him.

Alva crawled into an opening between the waterfall and the rocks to show them where to go and then popped his head back out.

"Em, you two better go through with me, so I can say the password."

Kay and Rob noticed the same green bubble that had engulfed the village houses now covering the base of the waterfall. Alva grabbed Kay and Rob's hands, pulling them through the opening and shouting, "Tansy!"

Kay had expected to be drenched by passing under the water, but to her surprise she was as dry as she had been before entering.

"I'm not wet!" Kay uttered, feeling her clothes.

"The bubble is waterproof, because getting wet is dangerous for Nymphas. If we do, our magic dust can wash off and then we won't be able to do any magic," he explained.

Kay and Rob looked around them. They were standing in

a hollow, where a few large flowers and miniature leaves were scattered on the ground.

"You had better stay here until morning. Nobody will know you're here, so make yourselves at home."

Rob approached the flowers and settled down on the petals. At once, the petals folded over him.

"This is actually quite cosy," Rob said as he snuggled up to sleep.

Kay ventured to the next flower and sat within it. The flower was gentle, hugging her like her mother did so often. She thought of her mother, how worried she must be. How was she to explain everything that had happened?

Alva turned to them before leaving.

"Remember, just say "Tansy" if you want to get by the enchantment, okay?" Alva reminded them.

"Okay," Kay said sleepily.

"Goodnight," whispered Alva as he left the falls.

Kay trusted that Alva would be back in the morning to show them home, but she was worried about her mother. They couldn't risk going back though; Harron might still be waiting, or worse. They would be much safer going back in daylight.

Kay felt so tired now and Rob had already fallen asleep. Kay closed her eyes, but she thought only of her mother and how worried and upset she'd be until, eventually, she fell fast asleep.

Chapter 6
-The Falls-

The sounds of rushing water, unfamiliar bird calls and Rob's loud snoring caused Kay to wake from her peaceful sleep. The flower released her at the first movement of her body and Kay arose, approaching the rushing water.

We need to get back to Mum, Kay thought anxiously.

"Tansy," Kay said as she leapt past the falls, into the woods.

The forest was even more enchanting by day and Kay smiled happily at the magnificent scene. The grass and flowers were almost as tall as her and swayed back and forth, like waves in the ocean. The trees moved as well, swatting at creatures that came too close. Oversized mushrooms grew at the foot of the trees, in dazzling shades of pink, blue and red.

Kay bounded up to a patch of flowers at the edge of the clearing where an unusual bug lay on multi-coloured petals. The bug was long, bright blue and had dragonfly wings, with six horse-like legs. When Kay approached, it flew into the trees and Kay followed. The insect bounded along the tops of many spotted toadstools as Kay chased it, until eventually it landed on the ground and galloped into the darkness. At that point Kay stopped, spotting a light in the gloom. One of the trees had a long, slender twig, glowing in the darkness. Kay ventured closer, but something moved and she saw an animal with four bright eyes watching her in the darkness. Kay backed away from the creature. She turned and ran as fast as she could, back towards the waterfall. When she reached out of the trees, she looked around to see if anything was following her but found nothing. Kay heard a yell coming from the other side of the waterfall and realised her brother was trapped behind it.

"Don't worry, Rob, I'm here!" Kay shouted back, running over to the gap between the rushing water.

Rob was peering out of the hollow.

"How'd you get out there?" Rob shouted.

"I said the password and it let me through." Kay raised her foot, calling "Tansy!" and landed right in front of Rob.

"Ouch!" Rob yelled, as Kay landed on his foot.

"Sorry!" Kay gasped.

"Watch where you're putting your feet," Rob growled, hobbling around. "What's the password?"

"It's Tansy," Kay said, grabbing Rob's arm. "C'mon, let's go, it's brilliant out there."

Both Kay and Rob jumped out of the falls and Rob saw all the insects, flowers and animals that roamed around the water.

"We're in the fairy world, aren't we? It wasn't just a dream," Rob said.

Kay laughed, peering up at a strange fruit that had sprouted from the trees. The fruit was red and shiny, like an apple, but it was pear-shaped. Kay climbed the tree and picked it off. She was about to take her first bite when something knocked her down. Kay felt dizzy as she sat up to find a large bug in front of her. She screamed as it bounded on top of her. Rob grabbed a stick from the ground and swung at the bug, causing it to leap into the air with a piercing screech. Kay jumped up and grabbed a stick too, holding it pointed towards the beast. The creature cowered, looking frightened by the sticks, and Rob charged at the giant bug. A blast of blue magic shot him backwards and he fell beside Kay. Kay looked around to find Alva flying towards them.

"What are you doing?" he shouted with fury. "That's my pet, you don't hurt her!"

The dog-sized insect bounded up to Alva and jumped around with excitement.

"She's only a cricket!" Alva said, sighing with relief when he realised, she was unharmed.

"*That's* a cricket?" Kay called with surprise. "It knocked me down!" She was still in shock at seeing her brother collapsed on the ground. "Look at what you've done to my brother!" she gasped.

"Well, at least I wasn't going to kill your brother!" Alva shouted back.

"Sorry, we didn't know she was yours!" Kay said, helping her brother up.

"That's your *pet*?" Rob said, gasping for breath as he struggled to get up. Alva nodded. "Well, it almost killed Kay," Rob said, scowling at the giant cricket.

"Is this yours?" Alva asked, picking up the fruit.

Kay saw that the fruit she had picked had turned black in colour.

"This is a Mort, one of the most poisonous fruits in Edenland. You're lucky, Tansy saved your life."

Kay felt a bit ashamed.

"You should've waited for me before touching anything," Alva warned. "C'mon, let's just put this behind us and I'll show you what's safe and what's dangerous."

Kay walked over to the cricket and patted her on the head; the insect bounced in circles with excitement. Rob was still a little wary of the giant bug but kept close as they all wandered into the trees.

Kay, Rob and Alva exited the woods near a gigantic bush surrounded by a large river which was called the Ever River. The bush was at least sixty feet high and it contained many ripe strawberries the size of small houses.

"This is my school," Alva said, gesturing towards the bush.

"I wish *our* school was a strawberry bush," Rob muttered, gazing at all the delicious fruit.

"Well, it's almost time for school," Alva notified them.

"So, how can you go to school in a bush?" Kay asked.

"Well, the strawberries are the classrooms, you see," Alva explained, and then looked at the ring on his thumb as a voice suddenly spoke.

"Alva… Alva?" the ring called.

Tansy gave a chirp at the sound of the voice.

"Oh, that's my mum calling me on my Tactus ring," Alva told them as he wandered away from Kay and Rob, speaking to the ring on his thumb.

"Hi, Mum. Yes, I'm at school…" The conversation continued but faded into a drone as Alva walked farther away.

Tansy gave a chirp at the sound of the voice. Alva wandered away from Kay and Rob, speaking to the ring.

"Hi, Mum. Yes, I'm at school…" The conversation continued but faded into a drone as Alva walked farther away.

Kay heard voices coming from the trees behind them.

"Quick, Rob, hide, someone's coming!"

Kay nudged her brother and then they hid behind a small

bush.

Kay and Rob peered over their bush to find other Nympha children, walking down the rainbow path to the school. All of them had bright yellow hair, two thumbs and toes, and pointed ears. The only difference that Kay could see was that some of the Nymphas had silver wings and some had gold. Kay and Rob watched on as they all travelled towards the school. Alva came out from behind the nearest tree.

"That was my mum," Alva announced. "I couldn't let her see you."

At that moment, a strange noise came from the school. It sounded like the squawk of a bird, but Kay took it to be the school bell.

"I'm late; we need to get going," declared Alva.

"Where are *we* going to go?" asked Rob with concern.

"You're going to hide in the school; I know a place," replied Alva.

Alva sent Tansy home, then they entered the school after everyone else had gone inside. Kay and Rob climbed the branches with difficulty while Alva hovered above them all the way to the "sixth floor". They entered an empty strawberry classroom and Alva sent golden glitter into the air from his wrists, and it floated up Kay and Rob's noses.

"No one comes in here because it's rotting, but you won't smell it because of the spell. Right, I've got to go, so stay here and don't come out until I come back for you, okay?"

"What about our Mum, Alva? She'll be wondering where we are!" Kay panicked.

"Yeah, can't you ditch school and take us back to *our* world?" Rob quizzed him, but Alva shook his head.

"It's not safe. The Portal is guarded by day. It won't be

good if you two are spotted. I don't want any trouble, so stay here until I come back for you, okay?" Alva repeated, and Kay and Rob nodded.

Alva vacated the strawberry classroom and Kay looked around. She walked over to where there was a hole for the window. Glancing out, she saw a breathtaking view that was nothing like the scene from *her* classroom. Below the school window was the river, sparkling up at her, and beyond the trees she spotted the village, looking like little green washing-up liquid bubbles. Kay looked to her right and saw a gathering of enormous trunks, much taller than the strawberry bush. It stood in the centre of a well-kept garden that had many animals patrolling its walls. The branches had flags bearing elaborate crests and Kay knew the trunk was a castle.

"Look, Rob, you can see everything up here!" Kay said excitedly.

Rob was already behind her, gazing at the view; he was interested in the castle too.

"I wonder what those monsters are," Rob said, peering down into the castle gardens.

"Alva will be able to tell us when he gets back," Kay said.

"What if we get caught in here and those fairies start shooting magic at us?" Rob said anxiously.

"Well, we've just got to trust that Alva knows what he's doing," Kay said, pacing around the room.

As she moved, giant leaves started to spring from the floor. They sprouted level with her waist and shaped themselves as seats. Toadstools then sprouted up in front of them.

"Rob, these are their desks and seats!" Kay guessed.

The leaves had risen around the edges of the classroom,

leaving a space in the centre for some other purpose. Kay sat down and smiled, thinking, *Margaret can't get to me here.*

"Kay… we've spent too long here. We need to get back to Mum," Rob told her anxiously, and he rushed towards the door to leave the classroom.

-Chapter 7-
The Woodburn Trio

"Don't, Rob!" Kay warned him. "We should wait for Alva to come back."

"I'm done with waiting. We need to get back to Mum," Rob told her as he opened the door.

Rob sneaked into the branch-like corridor and Kay followed him out. They saw many strawberry classrooms and Kay couldn't help taking a peek around one of the doors.

She saw all of the class in their seats at the sides, while one pupil and the teacher stood in the centre. Kay saw the pupil sprinkle her magic dust from her wrists towards a bug-like creature buzzing in the air. The creature appeared to fall asleep and the class cheered for the girl. Rob grabbed Kay's arm.

"C'mon, Kay, let's go."

"Look, Rob! They're casting spells."

Rob took a peek and became interested in what he was seeing too. Nympha after Nympha stood up to test their skills and spell after spell was repeated on the beast.

"Kay, look, it's Alva and he's up next!" Rob said, leaning in closer to the door.

Kay watched Alva repeat the same incantations and receive a cheer.

"Boo!" shrieked a voice from behind them, causing Kay and Rob to jump.

They swiveled around to find three Nymphas standing in front of them, two girls and one boy. They looked slightly like Alva, but they all had silver wings instead of gold.

"Look, Holly, they don't have wings, they can't be Nymphas!" squeaked the smaller of the girls, eyeing them up and down. She had long yellow hair that was tied up with a vine-like material.

"Maybe they're Imps," spat the taller girl, who had long straight hair that fell around her face.

The boy was the smallest of the three, with untidy hair and grubby clothes.

"Who are you?" the boy said sharply, as Kay and Rob backed away from them.

Kay noticed that they all wore the same type of leaf clothing.

Kay turned to Rob.

"If we had stayed where we were supposed to, we wouldn't have been caught!" she growled to him.

"Keep your voice down, whoever you are," whispered the tall girl. "Someone will hear you!"

"So you're hiding too?" Rob quizzed them.

"Yeah, we're skipping class," said the boy. "What *are* you?"

"We're Humans," said Kay.

"Shhh!" whispered Rob.

"Cool, we found Humans!" said the boy excitedly.

"Come away from the door, we'll find some other place to hide," the tall girl said.

All of them went outside the school.

"Can we get back to the rotten classroom before your school finishes?" Kay asked, remembering Alva.

"Yeah, sure, why?" said the tall girl, eager to know everything.

"Well, we need to meet Alva, so he can take us home," said Kay, thinking of her mother.

"You know Alva?" the boy asked.

"Yes, he brought us here, he's our friend," Kay told him.

"Alva's your friend?" replied the boy, sniggering.

"Why are you laughing?" asked Rob.

"No reason. It's just, Alva's a bit of a know-it-all," said the tall girl. "He's also told on us countless times and spoiled our fun."

"Were you doing wrong?" Kay asked, and she gave a mischievous grin.

"We like our fun; we're the rebels of the village. We're not losers like the rest of the do-gooders in class!"

"What's wrong with doing well?" Kay said, starting to think they had made a mistake following them outside.

"Nothing, never mind." The tall girl shrugged. "So, what are your names? I'm Holly."

"I'm Rob and this is my sister, Kay," Rob said, gazing at her.

"I'm Fern," said the boy.

"And I'm Ivy," squeaked the smaller girl.

Fern flew up to one of the trees and then gave a fruit to Kay.

"It's a Panapple, the sweetest fruit you'll ever eat in Edenland," he said, smiling broadly.

Kay looked at the gift as though it were poison, remembering the last fruit she had picked. The fruit was the colour of a banana but the shape and feel of a carrot. She took a bite and everyone paused while she did so.

The fruit tasted like a pear at first but then became sweeter, like a red grape. "That was delicious!" Kay said with delight.

All three Nymphas took to the air and brought bundles of the fruit down so they could enjoy a feast.

After eating over five Panapples, Kay was full and wanted to explore Edenland with the triplet Nymphas. The triplets called themselves the "Woodburn Trio" because Woodburn was their second name.

"What do you wanna do?" asked Ivy.

Holly looked over toward the castle.

"Why don't we spy on old Edwin?" she said mischievously.

"What's the fun in that?" asked Ivy.

"Well, we could give him a bit of grief," Holly replied, widening her eyes.

Ivy gave a grin and then looked with anticipation for her brother's agreement. Everyone turned to Fern and Kay realised he had been watching her.

"All right then, but we better not get caught or Dad will kill us," said Fern, sighing.

"Yes!" Ivy hissed, leaping into the air and fluttering back down.

Kay, Rob and the Woodburn Trio all wandered up to a giant wall of large grass blades that extended around the castle gardens. Each blade of grass had a face that showed no kindness.

"What are you all doing here? You're not welcome unless you have an appointment with the king!" said one of the grass blades grumpily.

Ivy sprinkled the gold dust from her wrists and shouted,

"Bitty!" The magic swirled around four of the grass blades, shrinking them to knee height. At once, the other grass blades turned ferocious, growing spikes like cacti. They slammed their bodies forwards and bumped into one another to guard the gardens.

"We don't need to go that way!" called Fern, grabbing Kay with his thumbs and lifting her into the air by the strength of his wings.

They flew over the grass and onto the other side. Holly carried Rob, while Ivy landed first in the castle gardens on a broad patch of flowers. The flowers towered above them all, but Kay and Rob could see the tree trunk castle up ahead.

"What's the castle called?" asked Kay.

"It's Evertrunk Castle," Holly told them.

"What's that?" shouted Rob, pointing at large beasts with Nymphas riding on their backs.

"Trouble!" called Fern, crouching lower. "Serpenduos."

The beasts had two green snake heads, with large fangs and forked tongs appearing and disappearing within their mouths. They walked on two bird legs and dragged behind them gigantic snake tails slithering from side to side, whilst flapping tiny chicken wings in the air for balance. The Nymphas sat on the backs of the beasts' feathered chicken bodies, wearing matching uniforms. Kay suddenly got a bad feeling that they would get in great trouble for this.

"I don't like this; we should get out of here!" Kay whispered in panic to the rest, as they watched the guards and their monsters approaching.

"Yeah, we'll get out of here… right after we have our fun!" Holly said, cackling quietly.

She aimed her wrist at the creature, whispering,

"Tanglet." Giant shreds of elastic material flew through the air, entangling around the Serpenduos' legs. The creatures gave screaming cries and hit the ground with a thud. Ivy then sprang into the air, shouting names at the guards. All the guards who saw her flew after her, shooting spells and screaming incantations. Holly, Fern, Kay and Rob were then free to sneak around, exploring the grounds. They approached the castle, peering into its windows, and Fern opted to be the lookout while the others examined the inside of the castle.

Within the castle's outer wall was another garden, filled with all sorts of exotic plants, formed as furniture, and large busts of Nymphas carved from stone.

"Quick! Someone's coming!" Fern called and all of them hid in the nearest giant flower bed.

Kay spotted Ivy flying in their direction.

"Hey, you, stay where you are!"

One of the guards had spotted her, but Ivy flew for the flowerbed. The guard shouted a spell and hit Ivy. She crashed into the short grass and the guard began moving in. Holly rose up above the flowerbed and shot a spell at the guard.

"Bitty!" she shouted, causing the guard to shrink to the size of a rat. She swooped down to rescue her sister but it was too late; more guards had already encircled her.

"Look! Another one!" shouted a guard, aiming an implement at Holly.

He didn't shoot golden Nympha Dust from his wrists; a long, wooden finger was there instead, sparkling at the tip. The guard shouted an incantation and the finger shot a lightning bolt towards Holly. The spell just missed her and she dashed back to the flowers, out of breath.

Guards flew in from all directions and tried to surround

them. Holly and Fern were the first to make a break for it as spells started shooting everywhere. Rob snatched Kay's hand and they both ran after Holly and Fern, but the Nymphas flew over the giant grass wall, leaving Kay and Rob behind.

Kay heard someone call, "Flam!" and at once she and Rob were surrounded by a ring of fire. Kay didn't know what to do. She and Rob started screaming as the fire wall closed in on them.

-Chapter 8-
King Edwin

"Help!" Rob called over the fire.

"We can't fly, we're Human!" Kay wept.

They heard a few voices shouting and a shower of water fell over the fire, causing it to go out. A Nympha guard glared down at them. He spun Rob around and examined him.

"Hey, stop that!" Rob shouted, but the Nympha ignored him and did the same to Kay.

"Yep, they're both Human!" the guard called to the others.

The Serpenduo tried to lunge at Kay and Rob, but the guards restrained them.

"Come with us," the lead guard ordered.

The Nympha guards took them within the castle and into the main hall. Ivy was carried in too.

An enormous plant was situated in the middle of the hall, with straight and narrow leaves. The plant stretched as high as the castle ceiling and had three giant white roots that lay on the floor in front of them, each with coloured tips.

The guards moved everyone onto one of the large flat roots and it moved upon command. Steadily, it stretched all the way to the top floor. The white root came to a halt and rolled its end to become part of the floor. They all marched onwards down many corridors, until they came to a wide room that had copper-coloured flowers climbing the bark walls. The next room was the last; they stood before a throne made of stone. The seat was highly decorated with creatures Kay didn't recognise.

Sitting on the throne was an old Nympha, wearing a crown that sparkled like the stars at night. He had straggly, dim, yellow hair that dropped to his waist. His face was creased with wrinkles, and a long beard hung from his chin down to his big-toed feet as he sat. His body was hunched and his head tilted as he sat on the throne's mossy seat.

He looked at Kay and Rob curiously and suspiciously, before clambering down from his high throne, swishing his cloak made of autumn leaves. Kay noticed the king had only three wings, like his statue.

"You're Humans!" he gasped, astonished at the sight of them both. "How did they get into Nymphas' World?" he demanded, turning to his guards furiously.

The guards explained how they had caught them in the gardens and that Holly and Fern had got away. King Edwin looked from one to the other and then focused on Kay.

"How did you get here?" he asked Kay slowly, as though she might have trouble understanding him.

"Don't tell him, Kay, he might kill us!" Rob shouted frantically, trying to escape the grip of the guard holding him.

"Do you not like Humans, Your Majesty?" Kay asked softly, peering innocently up at him.

King Edwin grinned, as though the situation was no longer serious.

"Now, that's not the point, Human; all I want to know is how you got here," he said, keeping the smile upon his lips.

"What are you going to do with us?" Kay asked, as she watched her brother wriggle out of the guard's reach and rush to stand beside her.

"We're not going to hurt you; you're quite welcome here as far as I'm concerned," King Edwin said to all of the room. "But it is not me you should be concerned about," the king whispered darkly. "There are others who might want to kill you."

"You mean the Onyx?" Kay guessed, remembering what Alva had said.

"Clever. Did a Nympha bring you here?" the king enquired suspiciously.

"Why, will he get in trouble?" Kay gasped, frightened of what was going to happen.

"So, it wasn't Ivy... another child brought you here?" interrogated the king.

"No," Kay squeaked.

"Who, then?" the king asked.

"Will the fairy, I mean Nympha, who brought us here, get in trouble? He was only saving us from bullies and..."

"My dear child, no harm will come to him... what kind of king do you think I am?"

"I don't know, I've never met a king before," Kay responded.

The king looked taken aback by Kay's response.

"I only want to save you both from harm," he said anxiously, turning to Rob.

Rob considered the king for a moment.

"We came through a portal," he said.

"Yes, the Portal, the one in Elna Wood?" the king said, his face lighting up with interest.

"Well, it was the one before the village, with big statues nearby."

"Whoever led you here was quite foolish, but you'll have to hide with him tonight, so the Onyx Nymphas don't find you. Who knows what they'll do if they find Humans in Edenland."

The king paused, deep in thought.

"Was it Dandy Roundale who brought you here?"

"No," Rob said, looking confused.

Kay happened to glance at her feet and saw that the floor was a giant sundial, and the time on the dial told her that it was late in the day. She thought of Alva — he was still at school, and they were supposed to have stayed there to meet him.

"We need to meet him!" Kay cried to Rob.

"What's the time? Has the school ended yet?" Rob asked in a panic.

"Why, is the Nympha going to meet you there?" the king questioned curiously.

"Yes, we need to meet Alva!" Kay said, annoyed that the king always replied to their questions with more questions.

The king pondered some more.

"Alva... Alva Cumber?" he guessed.

"I suppose so," Kay said, shrugging. "Do you know him?"

"My dear, I know everyone in Ever... it is my duty to know them," he said, his face full of astonishment. "Well," he added, looking to the large sundial, "the school day is about to end. You had better hurry and catch him."

Kay and Rob were relieved that the king wasn't mad with them or Alva.

"My guards will personally escort you both and Miss Woodburn off the premises and back to the school."

He gave a nod to the guards and they all turned to leave.

"But, children, make sure you leave as soon as you can, we don't want any trouble," the king added.

Kay, Rob and Ivy were led back to the school by the guards, and they entered the strawberry bush.

"I can't believe we got caught. What did you tell him?" Ivy asked.

"We told him how we got into Edenland. Is that bad?" asked Kay.

"Yeah, it might be; did he want you here?" Ivy asked.

"No," Kay replied sadly.

"Then he probably wants to keep your lot out," Ivy told them matter-of-factly.

Kay and Rob climbed the branches of the school, with Ivy flying beside them, her wings whirring rapidly. They departed from Ivy and went straight for the rotting classroom. They found that Alva was already there.

"Where have you been? You were supposed to wait here!" Alva shouted frantically.

"That's what I told her, but she wouldn't listen to me!" Rob said, pointing his finger at Kay.

"What! It was you who left the classroom first!" Kay argued. "I wanted to go back, but then other Nymphas came and…"

"Other Nymphas!" Alva growled.

There was a moment's silence and Kay and Rob glanced at each other in disgrace.

"What other Nymphas?" Alva groaned, trying to calm down.

Kay thought her next answer was going to make him even more furious; however, she had to reply.

"The Woodburn Trio," she piped up, gulping.

"What! You met three of the most badly behaved Nymphas in the school!" he shouted. "No doubt they got you

72

into trouble?" he added.

Rob nodded and Alva frowned at them both. He was now waiting on the story, ready to tell them off again.

"Well?"

"Well, it was Kay's fault, running out of the room when I told her that you'd be mad..." Rob lied.

"That's not true! It was you who left the room!" Kay defended herself.

"Forget who went out first. You both left when I told you not to!" Alva snapped and then Kay piped down. "Just... tell me what happened?" he asked exasperatedly.

Rob then told the whole story and Alva grew angrier as the story went on. Kay wanted to interrupt when it felt too one-sided, but she was silenced by Alva's hand every time.

"So, the triplets know about you and so does King Edwin, not to mention countless guards and trees that could tell the Onyx Nymphas where you are!"

"The king said we should stay at your house, but we need to get back to our mum..." Kay said.

"Yes... the king's right. If the Onyx know about you being here, they'll be guarding the Portal. You'll need to stay at my place where my family can protect you."

"But we can't stay, our mum will be worried sick about us," Kay cried, with Rob nodding in agreement.

"It's too dangerous at the moment. I'll ask my mum what to do," Alva decided.

"Okay," Kay and Rob muttered glumly.

Alva led Kay and Rob back towards the village in silence. They trekked through the forest again to remain unseen by other Nymphas, but the trees jeered and shouted at them to leave Edenland. Alva recognised one of the trees, that looked much friendlier.

"Slumber, you're awake!" he said, sounding cheerful again.

"Alva!" the tree replied with a booming voice that shook the forest floor.

"Kay, Rob, I'd like you to meet Slumber. He's barely ever awake, so you're lucky," Alva said with a chuckle.

"So, how long has it been then?" Slumber asked.

"At least two years!" answered Alva, looking pleased to see his old tree friend.

Slumber looked a little confused, eyeing Alva up and down.

"That long, eh... so have I ever met you before?" Slumber asked, turning to Rob.

Rob quivered a little, replying to the tree, "No."

"They're Humans, Slumber," Alva explained.

"Humans in Edenland!" the old tree gasped, widening his large eyes. "But that's impossible; Humans can't see the Great Rowan Tree. Unless a Nympha opened their eyes to her!"

"Yes, Slumber, I let them in. They were in trouble, so I let them hide in Edenland."

"But Alva, the Onyx Nymphas! They'll kill them, if they get the chance."

"I know, Slumber, that's why I need your help. Your roots can take us into the village. We can get to my house safely from..."

A great screech sounded above them. Alva grabbed Kay and Rob, dragging them to the ground. A giant bat circled the area with a strange creature riding on its back. Suddenly, the bat swooped down in their direction. Alva panicked.

"Slumber, your roots, hurry!" he cried to the tree.

The tree lifted his roots like a straggly dress, dirt crumbling from the bottom. Kay, Rob and Alva dived beneath, hearing the sounds of trees wailing and screaming, "The Humans went that way!"

Alva hoisted Kay and Rob up from the floor of the roots.

"C'mon, they know you're both here now!" he said.

Alva led them through twisting corridors of roots and down earthy chutes. Kay felt smaller and looked around at Rob, noticing that he had shrunk also.

"I think it's this way," Alva said, pointing to a root.

"You 'think'," groaned Rob. "You mean you don't know where we're going?"

"It's been two years; can you remember everywhere you've been?" Alva retorted. "You're lucky we're even here!" he said.

Rob and Kay, out-argued again by the Nympha, followed him in silence.

-Chapter 9-
The Cumbers

After pacing around the roots of Slumber for over an hour, Alva finally admitted they were lost.

"Now what do we do?" Rob groaned.

Kay's feet were aching and blistered from walking. She regretted ever leaving the classroom — now she and her brother were being hunted by creatures of little mercy.

Alva had a silver leafed pouch that formed from the garments on his chest and dropped out onto his hands. Kay had noticed that the straps to the pouch hooked around his neck, but the pouch itself could appear and disappear into his clothes. Alva whispered, "Tansy" to the little bag, and it sprung open. He began rummaging inside and pulled out an object that looked quite like a large rabbit's ear. He attached it to the belt of his clothes and Kay stared at it.

"It's a Catalop's ear," he informed Kay. "We'll know if there's danger up ahead, if this twitches."

He then fastened the two vine strings on his pouch and it disappeared back into his clothes, out of sight.

"I think it's about time I told my mum about you two," Alva said.

He wandered a few feet away, looking closely at his ring. It was silver with an oval-shaped orange stone in the middle. Around the outside of the stone were miniature golden petals that moved when Alva spoke to it.

"Mum... Mum, can you hear me?"

"Alva, where have you been? I've been so worried! No one could tell me where you were or... where are you anyway?"

"It's okay Mum, I'm in Slumber's roots and we're heading for the village," Alva answered to reassure her.

"We — who else is with you? I bet you their parents will be worried sick too!"

"Well, Mum, that's sort of what I want to talk to you about. The two that are travelling to the village with me are Humans."

Alva waited for a response and Kay and Rob edged in closer.

"Humans?" quizzed the voice, sounding a little more anxious.

Alva turned to Kay and Rob, holding the ring in front of Kay. She saw a little face within the stone which she guessed to be Alva's mother. She had the same yellow hair as all the other Nymphas Kay had seen, but it was bushy and bounced around when she moved her head. She looked curious as she peered up at Kay. For a moment she looked a little confused, but then she put on a merry smile.

"So *you're* the Humans the whole village is talking about?" she said with excitement.

"Mum, this is Kay the Human. Kay, this is my mum," Alva said before turning the ring in Rob's direction. "Mum, this is Rob the Human. Rob, this is my mum."

Alva turned the ring to himself again.

"We're a bit lost. Can you send someone to come find us?"

"Of course, dear, I'll send Dandy; he knows those old roots like the veins on his wings!"

"Thanks Mum!" Alva beamed at the ring and then he rubbed it, causing her face to disappear. "Okay then, we'll just need to wait until Dandy gets here."

"Who's Dandy?" Rob asked nervously.

"Don't worry, he's a Nympha; my family's been friends with him for years."

*

The wait was endless; Kay and Rob wondered when Dandy was going to appear. They distracted themselves by asking Alva questions on the Magic of Nymphas' World.

"So, can you really turn yourself invisible?" Rob said with excitement.

"No. If you eat a Baca fruit you can camouflage yourself, like I did. To turn yourself completely invisible you need Snow Cream, but it grows far away in a place called Ater. The only other way you could turn invisible is if it's one of your gifts."

"Do you mean like a special ability?" asked Kay curiously.

"Yes. I'm talking about the Seven Gifts."

Kay and Rob edged closer, their interest peaked. Alva continued to explain.

"Well, as I said, there are seven Gifts: the Gift of Touch, the Gift of Sight, the Gift of Flight, the Gift of Speech, the Gift of Growth, the Gift of Knowledge and the Gift of Mysteries. The Gift of Touch is when you grow Dustlits," he lifted his arms to reveal the golden patches on the underside of his wrists, "that's when you can begin to learn your own magical strengths."

"But, how did you *get* it?" Rob asked impatiently.

"Well, I think it's different for every Nympha, but I got mine by touching one of the statues in Elna Wood."

"So, what other gifts do *you* have?" Kay questioned, wanting to know more.

"Well, I also have the Gift of Sight, the Gift of Flight and the Gift of Speech. The Gift of Flight is when your wings appear; I got mine when I went beyond the school into Catalops' Meadow. I got the Gift of Speech when I started learning the ancient language of the Nymphas and Tansy spoke to me. When I first learned the ancient language, Tansy spoke to me. When I replied, I soon realised I was able to talk to all sorts of insects. Different Nympha races have different Gifts of Speech. Only really powerful Nymphas can talk to reptiles and amphibians though. Their language is extremely difficult. King Edwin can talk to reptiles; in fact, he's even got an enormous tortoise in his castle gardens."

"What about the Gift of Sight?" Rob asked.

"Well, I gave you two the Gift of Sight to see the Rowan Tree. I got the Gift of Sight when I first ventured out of the village and drank the Ever River's water."

The Catalop's ear began to twitch out of control as a shadow appeared around the corner.

"Dandy!" Alva roared with delight, bounding over to him.

"Hello there, Alva, your mother told me you were in a bit of trouble," Dandy grinned. "And Humans in Nymphas' World, who'd have thought!" he said, scratching his head of straggly, long hair. His face was extremely friendly-looking as his tall and lanky frame strode up to Kay and Rob, smiling and shaking their hands.

"Hello, I'm Dandy and I'm very pleased to meet you!"

"You! You're the one that the king was talking about; he thought *you'd* led us here," Rob said accusingly.

"Yeah, well, let's just say it wouldn't be the first time I've saved a creature from Earth by leading it here, but Humans..." He turned to Alva. "You do realise I'll still get in trouble for this!"

"Why's that, Dandy?" Alva asked in confusion.

"Well, Old Edwin will think that I showed you how to do it, won't he?" he said, with a slight smile and a twinkle in his eye.

Alva, Kay and Rob followed Dandy out of the tree's roots. When they climbed through the exit, Kay felt herself grow again, back to her normal size. She found that they were in the middle of the village and all around them were the giant green bubbles, glinting in the sunlight.

"Okay, Alva, I'll be leaving you now," Dandy said, patting his back. "You all watch yourselves and keep away from Onyx Nymphas!" he added as he walked away in the other direction.

"Right, we've got to hurry," Alva told them, beckoning them to follow his lead.

They dashed past most of the bubbled houses, keeping to the stony rainbow-coloured path. Alva finally came to his house and they approached the bubble.

"It'll probably be better if we go in one at a time. The password is 'Amos'. Okay?" Both of them nodded.

Alva went through the bubble first, whispering the password. The surface quickly swallowed Alva and he turned, from the other side, waving for Kay to come through. Kay gave a look to Rob then approached the bubble.

"Amos," she whispered and walked through.

Kay got a strange, tickly feeling when the bubble closed in on her and she noticed that the air became warm, like passing through the entrance of a supermarket. Rob followed suit and Alva led them to a potted plant that sat by his foxglove house.

"Hello Quizquil!" Alva said, addressing the plant.

Kay moved closer, inspecting the strange plant. It had four green petals, each with a razor-sharp tooth on the end. Its face, which consisted of two eyes, lay in the middle of the petals.

"Alva, where have you been? Your mother's been worried about you!" said the plant.

"I know, but we're okay now," Alva replied defensively. "Rob, Kay, this is Quizquil; he eats all our household garbage."

"What are they?" Quizquil asked, shriveling his eyes. "Humans!" he said with a hiss.

Kay and Rob hurried away from Quizquil and followed Alva to a large flower head, which he crawled into, like an insect searching for nectar. Kay and Rob clambered in as well, hearing the distant ramblings of the bin plant.

Once they had reached the top of the plant head, Kay felt herself shrink again. They approached the flower's stigma, that opened into a chute, which Kay realised was the plant's stem, growing from the depths. Alva gave them a sweet, reassuring smile, before sliding down the chute. Kay and Rob held onto one another as they jumped down it too.

Kay felt herself land softly on confetti-like petals that covered the floor of an odd chamber. Large petals shaped as chairs sprouted from the walls which were decorated with tiny flowers that changed colour and shape to form different patterns. Kay heard a familiar chirping noise from the next room and Tansy bounded up to meet them, happily dancing around Alva, Kay and Rob.

"Hi Tansy, where's Mum?" asked Alva. The cricket gave a few more chirps and Alva chirped back, before turning to Kay and Rob. "She's in the kitchen," he translated.

Kay and Rob waded through a sea of petals along a narrow corridor, while Alva and Tansy flew, buzzing above them.

In the middle of what Kay guessed to be the hall was a clearing, where a white root rose out of the floor. At the tip of the root there was a flat base with six large spots trimming the edges in colours of red, green, blue, purple, black and brown. Kay gazed around the hall at all the strange items, including the oval lights hovering near the ceiling.

Farther on was a room full of petals, like the hallway. This room however, had a large amber stone embedded in the ceiling. Continuing on, Alva led them past a room full of floating leaves and another that was closed by a leafed door. They then approached the last room of the house, which had steam creeping out from beneath the door.

"Hi, Mum!" Alva called, as they entered what Kay assumed to be the kitchen.

Kay and Rob looked around and saw that this room had five large flat-topped toadstools, each with brightly coloured food steaming on the top of them. Beside the toadstools was an enormous plant. Its roots were like tentacles as it moved across the floor and its vines picked utensils up and placed plates of food upon its massive leaves.

The Nympha they had seen in the ring was now standing in front of them, wearing a dress woven from the exact same material as that worn by all the other Ever Nymphas they had seen. As she turned towards them, her springy hair bobbed up and down above a slightly old-looking face, with a dazed expression that quickly turned into a smile as she saw her son.

"Happy birthday, son!" she squeaked, snatching Alva into a tight embrace and kissing the top of his head. "Look at you all, you're completely filthy. You'll need to visit the Dust Room. Alva, show them," she commanded, swerving back to attend to the dinner.

Alva showed them to the closed room they had walked by and flew up to the ceiling. He touched a large flower head, causing blue dust to sprinkle down upon them like soft, dry rain that disappeared as it hit the floor of the room. They saw all the dirt of the day fade and vanish.

After a few minutes, they all wandered out of the Dust Room, fresh and clean, to find two Nymphas standing in the hall. Alva ran up to greet them.

"Melvin… Merlin, you're home!" he called to them excitedly.

Kay recognised the Nymphas at once as being guards from the king's garden. They looked similar, except one was taller and more muscular than the other, with shorter hair. The shorter and thinner of the two, Alva called Melvin. He had saved Kay and Rob from the fire and explained to the king where he'd found them. Alva hugged Melvin.

"Happy birthday, Alva," Melvin said, hugging him back.

When Alva tried to hug Merlin though, Merlin didn't hug him back.

"Why did you bring Humans into Nymphas' World?" Merlin said sharply.

"They were in trouble, so they had to hide here," Alva said weakly.

"What? More trouble than a death sentence?" spat Merlin.

Alva looked down at his feet in shame and Kay felt guilty for the trouble she had caused. Alva's mum came around the corner.

"Now, we'll have no more of that. Dinner's ready," she said, flashing a smile to them all and then they went through to the dining room for dinner.

-Chapter 10-
Alva's Virga

The dining room was full of floating obstacles: a massive flower head that formed the table and leaf chairs that danced about the air. Alva flew Kay up to her seat, while Melvin helped Rob. Once they were all settled on the floating leaf chairs, the plant from the kitchen manoeuvred back and forth with steaming dishes, each placed on one of the table's petals.

"That's Kook, our Handy Plant," Alva told Kay as she stared at the fast-moving plant. Kay then stared at the table. The petals of the table had the names Alva, Merlin, Melvin, Jasmine and Amos engraved upon them. Kay thought Jasmine must be Alva's mother and she knew Amos was the family's house password, so Kay presumed Amos must be Alva's father.

Two extra placemats had been set down for Kay and Rob and Amos' seat remained empty. The food was served on hardened leaf plates brightly coloured in shades of red, blue and yellow. On Kay's plate was what looked like red beans swimming in an orange sauce. Next to them were long blue vegetables and a yellow type of meat, shaped like a sausage. Kay and Rob stared at their dinner; they had never seen anything like it.

"Is everything okay, dears?" Alva's mother asked, afraid that what she had cooked was not substantial.

Both Kay and Rob nodded and proceeded to eat the first bites of their food. Rob pulled faces whilst he ate. Kay tasted *her* food and found that the vegetables tasted unusually sweet. She tried the meat, tearing off a sliver, but as soon as the meat touched her tongue, she spat it back onto her plate and the Nymphas laughed. Kay had never tasted anything so revolting; it was like pure salt, sizzling on her tongue.

"I suppose you've got to have a Nympha's tongue for Pinkiwhirl meat!" Melvin laughed.

"What are *they*?" Kay choked.

"It's a small mammal from Feature Forest," Melvin replied with a smile.

After enjoying their first course, Kook the Handy Plant came through with a dessert.

"Now, Kay and... Bob, is it?" asked Alva's mother.

"Actually, my name's Rob," Rob said, a little embarrassed.

"Right, Rob and Kay!" she called, still smiling. "You have come on a special weekend. It's Alva's birthday today."

"Oh, and tomorrow's the Ever Celebration! Can they come with us, Mum? Please," Alva piped.

"Hmm, I don't think they should be going to the celebration, it's too dangerous!" said Alva's mother.

His brothers agreed, nodding their heads.

"But the Onyx *never* attend our celebrations!" Alva argued.

"Yeah, Alva, they'd only come to an Ever Day if there were Humans invited," Merlin added sarcastically, and his mother frowned.

"Yes... too dangerous," she repeated.

"You want to go see the celebration, don't you?" Alva

asked Kay and Rob.

Both of them stared at each other. Kay felt anxious as she knew they had already been too long away from their mother.

Alva's mother seized upon their hesitation to change the subject.

"Melvin, would you like to say a few words to mark Alva's birthday?" their mother prompted, turning to her eldest son.

He gave a nod and raised a stone-carved goblet.

"Alva, I would like to say congratulations on turning twelve and I hope your Virga serves you well in the future," he said, sipping from the goblet.

"Happy birthday, Alva," Kay and Rob cried in unison.

Everyone ate their dessert, consisting of colourful fruit in blue sauce. It was mouthwatering, so Kay finished the whole bowl.

"So, Kay... what is your mother like?" Alva's mother prompted.

"Eh... great. She'd do anything for us," Kay told her, missing her mother the more she thought of her.

Alva's mother smiled kindly, seeming to know her thoughts.

"She'll be awfully worried about you," she added with concern.

"Yeah, we really should be getting home," Rob mentioned, glancing at Kay.

"But what about the celebration? They'll miss it," Alva said, keen for Kay and Rob to go.

"Hmm," Alva's mother hummed, considering her son.

"C'mon Mum, you could do something about their mum, couldn't you, please?" Alva asked with puppy eyes, and his mother grinned.

"All right, I'll see what I can do," she conceded, and Merlin shook his head.

"You give in too easily, Mum. If it were me I'd say no is no," he told her, and she smiled wider.

"Would you now… are you trying to give me parenting advice, son?" She chuckled and Merlin blushed. "It *is* Alva's birthday, after all. I'll do it just this once," she added and then turned to Kay and Rob. "Now, write down your address."

Alva's mother pulled a leaf from the wall. She gave it to Rob and he looked at it blankly.

"What do I do with this?" he quizzed, and she chuckled.

"These are Letter Leaves. You can write on them with your thumbs," she explained and then pressed her thumb onto the green leaf, leaving a chalk-white mark.

Rob set to work, writing down his address with his finger. Kay thought it looked fun so she drew a smiley face after Rob had finished.

"Excellent. Tonight, I'll visit your mother and cast a spell to put her at ease," she told them, beaming.

"What are you going to do to her?" Rob asked, a little suspicious.

"Oh, nothing drastic, I'll just put her into a deep sleep. She'll sleep all day tomorrow and when she wakes, she'll think that it was all a dream. She'll forget you ever went missing and you'll both be back before she even wakes," she reassured them.

"Will it definitely work?" Kay asked.

"Of course, dear," she said, and beamed again.

After everyone had finished, they all got down from the floating chairs and table. The Nymphas looked excitedly at

Alva.

"Are you ready?" said Alva's mother to her youngest son.

"Yup, I've been waiting on this day a long time now!" Alva replied, heading towards the root in the middle of the hall. The rest of his family followed behind him.

Kay and Rob joined the Nymphas by the root and Alva climbed on and touched the brown spot. The root plunged beneath the floor and returned soon after, without Alva. The rest of his family did the same and Kay and Rob went down on the root together. The root whizzed past many hollows and Kay felt her stomach jolt as it suddenly halted in an underground barn. The barn was cavernous and they could hear the echoing sounds of animals, neighing and pawing the ground. Melvin shot a spell and stable doors swung open to reveal horse-like creatures. Alva whistled and one of the creatures trotted up beside him, bowing its head. It was like a silver Shetland pony, but slightly larger in stature, its body glistening in the dim light. As Kay drew nearer, she saw that it had no fur, save a long and flowing mane, also of silver. Its body appeared to be metallic, like liquid metal smoothly rippling with every flexing muscle. Alva flew up and gracefully landed on the pony's back.

"C'mon Kay, climb on my pony; you can ride with me," he called eagerly.

While Kay clambered onto the pony, Alva's family called their own ponies out, some silver and one the colour of copper.

"You can ride with me, Bob," said Alva's mother, awkwardly lifting Rob onto the pony.

Alva turned his pony, addressing his mother.

"What about Kay and Rob, Mum, it could be dangerous for them?"

"Oh, don't worry, Alva, we have Melvin and Merlin with us tonight. It's your birthday and a special one at that; don't let a few Onyx, ruin it."

At those words, Melvin shouted, "Aparta". The ground trembled, shifting an opening that the ponies ran through and out of the house's protective bubble.

"Off we go then!" Alva's mother called, and they all charged out of the village and into the dark forest.

"A... l... va... whe... re... a... re... we... go... ing?" Kay shouted into Alva's ear, as the pony bounded forward.

"I'm go... ing to get m... y pre... sent," Alva called back, leading the way through the darkness.

After riding for a while, they came to a stop in a small clearing. All was dark, but Kay could see a faint light glowing in the gloom. Alva wandered up to the light and Kay followed behind him. As she got closer, she saw that the light was a glowing twig, sticking out of a tree. Alva's family gathered around him.

"Ramulu," Alva began, addressing the tree.

The great fir tree shook her branches as she awakened, opening deep-set eyes on a friendly, crinkled face.

"Do you, Ramulu, give this Virga to me, Alva Cumber, to serve me all my life?"

"Yes, Alva Cumber, this Virga I give to you, to keep forever," echoed an old voice from the tree.

Alva snapped the twig off as gently as he could. It stopped glowing and its tip began to sparkle like a star. Alva bowed to the tree and she shook her branches as a new twig grew in place of the old.

Alva grinned to his family, each of them congratulating him and ruffling his hair.

"Wow, a wand!" Rob whispered to Kay.

"Well, see if it fits," Merlin encouraged him.

Alva slipped the twig into the patch on his wrist and it was slowly swallowed into his skin, with only the tip sticking out, like an extra finger. Alva smiled as he swished the twig around, leaving a trail of magical dust.

"Bitty," he shouted, pointing his Virga at a large mushroom.

The mushroom shrank slowly and all of Alva's family cheered.

"You'll get better with practice," Melvin said, patting his brother on the back.

Everyone returned to their ponies and galloped home. Kay, Rob and Alva retreated to the sitting room and collapsed among a sea of petals, resting their weary bodies. Kay gazed at her reflection in a great orange stone.

"Viva," Alva said in a lazy voice, pointing his Virga at the stone.

A Nympha's face appeared, telling them the latest news, and Kay realised the giant stone was like a television. Kay and Rob were fascinated by the stone, but Alva was busy trying out incantations on surrounding objects, making them shrink, float or grow bigger.

"Alva, can we go to bed now?" Kay asked, with a yawn.

"Sure!" Alva chirped as he stood up, stretching.

They wandered through to Alva's mother and she stared down at their exhausted expressions and smiled.

"You all look very tired; I think it's about time for bed," she said, walking over to the root in the hall.

Alva went first, touching the red spot and whizzing off to his room, calling goodnight as he disappeared. Alva's mother ushered Kay and Rob onto the root and stepped on behind them.

"Now, let me see: Duo... Novus... Conclav!" she said, tapping her Virga against the root.

Two other spots appeared on the root, one yellow and the other pink. The root gave a squirm and then settled again.

"I'm afraid your new rooms may be a bit cold, but I'll try my best to heat them." She then touched the yellow spot and their stomachs gave a jolt as the root dropped down the dark tunnel before stopping abruptly and zooming forwards. Kay felt as though she were on a rollercoaster ride.

"Here we are!" Alva's mother called as the root came to a halt. "Bob, this is your bedroom."

They all stepped into a tunnel, freshly carved from the soil. The tunnel led them to a leafed door and Rob opened it, unveiling a room carpeted with grass, bathed in light from many twinkling ovals. A large flower head lay in the centre and a chair-shaped petal sat next to the earthy wall. Rob lay on the flower head, assuming it to be the bed. It folded its petals around him and he gave a satisfied smile. Alva's mother started waving her Virga and chanting spells. Vines and flowers spread over the walls, blocking the drafts to make the room feel warmer. She also conjured up a cage that was clear, like glass, and then she called out of the room and an object came whizzing down the tunnel to meet her. It was a cocoon and she stuck her Virga inside and said: "Slumbus," before opening it. A large bug fell to the floor, unconscious. It was like a flying ant, but on the bottom of its abdomen were four lizard-like tails, each with a flap of skin on the ends. Alva's mother scooped up the insect and popped it into the cage. Rob looked a little frightened of the strange creature.

"Don't worry little one, it can't get out; it will keep you warm. Don't worry about your mother either. I'll have her sound asleep tonight as well," she promised.

With those words, she left Rob's room and Kay followed quickly behind her. They arrived back at the root and Kay prepared herself for another rollercoaster journey, but thankfully it was a short trip along the same tunnel.

"There we go," Alva's mother said, opening another leaf door.

It looked exactly the same as Rob's room. She called out the same enchantments and made yet another cage with a bug inside.

"Thanks for helping us... erm... Alva's mum," Kay said, as she lay on the flower head and its petals curled around her.

"No problem, dear; a friend of my son is a friend of mine, and you can call me Jasmine," she said, with a nod.

"Jasmine, are we going to the celebration tomorrow?" Kay asked sleepily.

"Yes, dear, we'll make sure you're safe. It'll be fun, and we'll leave early to get you two home to your mother. Yes, that way the Portal won't be guarded," Jasmine said, almost to herself. "I'll go to your mother now. Goodnight, Kay."

"Goodnight, Jasmine."

Jasmine pointed her Virga and whispered, "Obscura," causing the glowing stones on the ceiling to go out. She then closed the leaf door, leaving Kay to sleep.

Kay watched the cage in the darkness and saw sparks of fire igniting within as each of the insect's lizard-like tails turned to flames. Kay watched the insect hover in the cage and soon became warmed by its flames. The bug buzzed to and fro and, as Kay watched it, she drifted off to sleep.

Chapter 11
-The Silibis Plant-

Kay was awoken by Alva the next morning.

"Kay... Kay!" he called, entering the room.

"What time is it?" Kay mumbled.

Alva flew up and turned the glowing lights on.

"It's twenty minutes past eight," he replied.

"Eight!" Kay cried, slumping back down on the flower head bed.

"Sorry, is it too early for you?"

"A bit, yeah," she said, yawning and scratching her head.

Kay slipped out of bed and followed Alva to Rob's room.

"C'mon, Rob, let's go outside and I'll show you the village!" Alva said, but Rob turned the other way, hugging into one of his flower head's petals.

Alva winked at Kay and shot a spell at the bed. "Viva!" The flower jerked and spat Rob out, tossing him onto the soft grass.

"Okay, I'm up!" he growled.

Alva laughed. "That's what my mum used to do to me when I wouldn't get up for school."

Kay, Alva and Rob scoffed some tasty breakfast and laughed together at their messy faces covered in food. Kay was having so much fun with Alva and felt delighted to finally have a friend.

After breakfast, Kay and Rob ventured into the kitchen, following Alva. He stopped in front of a strange plant.

"This is a Silibis," Alva said, pointing to a large and unopened dark blue flower head. "I think it'll be safer if you disguise yourselves as Nymphas when we go outside, to avoid attracting the Onyx. If you take three bites of this flower, you will change into whatever you're thinking of at the time. So, if you're thinking of a fluffy Pinkiwhirl then it will turn you into one, so keep your minds focused. Okay, I want you to think of having wings; not just any wings, but Ever wings." He peeled off one of the flower's petals and handed it to Kay. "Take a bite."

Kay took a bite, forcefully swallowing it. It was disgusting! She tried to think only of having Ever wings. As she took her second and final bites, she got a strange feeling on her back.

"That's it, Kay, you've done it!" Alva squealed with delight.

Kay peered over her shoulder and giggled excitedly at the golden veined mayfly wings sprouting from her back. She still had red hair though.

"Right, now you, Rob," Alva instructed, giving him the same petal to eat.

Rob's face went sour and he looked as though he was about to spit it out.

"Rob, look at my wings, don't think of the flower or you'll turn into it!" Alva warned him.

Rob took his second bite and Kay could see his clothes start to break at the back and, as he took his last bite, the wings emerged, shaping into an exact replica of Alva's wings.

"Well done, Rob!" Alva said, patting his shoulder.

Rob looked pleased with himself, trying to take off, but clumsily fell over instead.

"They're not *real* wings, so you can't fly with them. They're only pretend, so you blend in. I'm going to walk beside you all the time so others don't get suspicious."

Rob looked cross that he couldn't fly, and Kay felt a little disappointed too. Alva was a bit worried about their hair not turning yellow, but it would have to do.

They all emerged from the house, passed through the protective bubble and started walking towards the centre of the village.

"Where are we going?" Kay asked.

"We're going to Dandy's shop," Alva announced.

"What's in his shop?" asked Rob excitedly.

"He sells all different kinds of creatures!" Alva said with a smile.

While they walked through the village, many Nymphas gave them funny looks and Alva began to get nervous.

On the way to Dandy's shop, Kay, Alva and Rob saw some familiar Nymphas.

"It's the Woodburns!" Kay whispered to Rob.

Alva quickly grabbed their arms and tried to divert them away, but it was too late.

"Hey, look, it's the Humans!" Fern called.

"Keep your voice down!" Alva spat at him.

"Oh yeah, remember, Fern, it's a secret," Holly said, grinning.

"Nice wings!" Ivy smirked at Kay and Rob, "The hair needs fixing though."

"Go away!" Alva growled at them.

"Don't be such a worrywart, Alva," Holly said, ruffling

his hair.

Alva knocked her hand away and pulled Kay and Rob in the other direction.

"You're not their keeper, Alva!" Fern called.

Alva spun back around to face Fern, who was a little smaller than Alva. He frowned at him and then he looked at Kay and Rob.

"Do you want to talk to these idiots?" Alva asked harshly.

"Not after they left us in the castle," Kay said, a bit scared to disagree with Alva.

"You see?" Alva said smugly.

"Shut up, Alva, we can talk to them if we want!" Holly snapped back.

Fern approached closer to Kay and Rob.

"We knew Old Ed wouldn't hurt you," he said.

Kay turned her back on them and marched away, feeling a little angry. Alva and Rob followed quickly behind her, leaving the Woodburns behind.

"I hate to admit it but the Woodburns are right. You look like strange Ever Nymphas without yellow hair," Alva commented, leading them to the outskirts of the village so they wouldn't be seen. However, the village was becoming busier now and Nymphas of all shapes and sizes were hovering about, forcing Alva, Kay and Rob to hide in the bushes

"This is never going to work," Alva moaned, watching every Nympha go by.

He noticed the Woodburn Trio hovering down the route and they stopped right in front of them.

"You can't hide from us," Holly cackled, peering down at them within the bushes.

"How'd you know we were here?" Rob demanded.

"Followed you, of course," Fern said, smirking.

"Why, you…" Alva piped up, trembling with fury.

"What I meant to say," Fern interrupted, "was that we can help you get along the road."

"What? Help us?" Kay asked, uncertain whether to trust them or not.

"Yes, help you. Look, I know we left you in the castle gardens, but we can make it up to you," Fern pleaded.

"How can *you* help us?" Alva scoffed at Fern. Fern thought hard.

"Well, we could cause a distraction or… I know! We could close off the path, say it's dangerous. Could work," Fern suggested, awaiting Alva's approval.

"You're just looking for trouble; you don't really want to help us," Alva whispered as someone else flew down the path. "Fine," he huffed, realising they were getting nowhere.

"I know a spell," piped up Holly. "Where are you heading?"

Alva frowned. He didn't want to tell Holly where they were going.

"We're going to Dandy's shop," Rob told Holly and Alva gave him a furious look. Holly smiled at Rob and he blushed.

Holly and her siblings flew to the end of the road and conjured a massive hedge stretching along the path beside Kay, Alva and Rob. They then started spouting elastic-like strands, weaving them together into a webbed roof connecting the hedge to the edge of the wood. Once completed, the Woodburn Trio looked pleased with their efforts and even Alva smiled at the tunnel they had created.

Kay, Alva and Rob made their way along the tunnel, listening to the confused chatter of the Nymphas on the path.

They soon reached the end of the tunnel, alighting at the far side of the village.

"Thanks for that," Kay said.

"Yeah, you're amazing," Rob added, looking at Holly. Holly blushed and Fern nudged his sister with a wink.

"I mean, you're all amazing," Rob added as his cheeks glowed red.

"We better go now or Dad won't be happy," Fern warned his sisters, and the girls nodded.

"Bye," squeaked Fern.

"Don't be a stranger!" Ivy chirped warmly, and then Holly ruffled Alva's hair again.

"See you around, Humans," she called out as she left, and Alva huffed as he sorted his hair.

"Stop saying they're Human!" he growled. Alva saw a crowd had gathered on the path with many Nymphas pointing angrily at the tunnel, so he grabbed Kay and Rob and raced towards Dandy's shop.

-Chapter 12-
Dandy's Shop

Dandy's shop was a geranium patch with a circle of blue stones surrounding a small hole in the centre of the ground. As soon as they stepped into the circle they shrank to the size of tiny mice, and the small hole became the gaping entrance to a sloping tunnel.

They made their way down the tunnel, which opened up to a large hollow. There were creatures everywhere, in cages and wandering around. Kay saw strange birds flying above her with red feathers and long tails, and in front of her were trees encased in bubbles, each with a creature on it. The first was like a koala with large bush baby eyes, its long tail coiled around the tree. Other creatures wandered freely and Kay noticed some of the creatures were from Earth.

"Dandy?" Alva called out, flying up and almost colliding with a bird. "There he is… Dandy!"

Kay heard Dandy respond over the racket of the animals and Alva landed back down. "He's coming; he's just feeding his Vola-tigris."

They heard a roar, which frightened even Alva, as Dandy appeared from behind a corridor of trees.

"Ah… Rob, Kay, nice wings… Silibis plant?" Dandy asked them, and Alva nodded. "Clever… So what do you think of the shop?"

"It's brilliant!" Rob said, gazing at all the wondrous creatures.

"You got this one from Earth," Kay said as a kitten wandered by. "Did you *steal* her?"

"Most of the creatures are wild, but yes, Kay, I did steal her, like many other Earth creatures in this store," Dandy replied sadly.

"Well, that's awful!" Kay exclaimed.

"Oh, no, Kay, that is not the awful part!" Dandy piped up. "You see, every creature I've have taken from Earth was hurt, starving or abandoned, just like your kitten there," Dandy explained. "I've brought them here to be respected and cared for," he said, bending down to pet the kitten.

"Oh... sorry, I didn't know," Kay said, feeling embarrassed.

"It's okay, I suppose I still thieve animals, but I do it with the best intentions," Dandy said, smiling. "Let me show you around!"

Kay saw many amazing creatures, some from Earth or similar to Earth animals and some beyond anything Kay could describe.

"I need to get back to work now," Dandy announced, once they had concluded their tour. "You see, one of the Serpenduos is expecting eggs and it's important for me to be there."

"Can we come too?" Rob asked, keen to see more.

"I suppose," Dandy said, gesturing towards a nearby root, similar to the one in Alva's house.

They each ventured down the root, and Kay could hear the shrieking of the Serpenduo getting louder. The root halted and Kay was confronted by ferocious creatures, each with two green snake heads, a snake tail and bony legs beneath a giant feathery body of either white or golden plumage. The first beast was standing, back arched, looking down upon them curiously, its four large snake eyes reflecting Kay's fearful face. It made a sudden jerking movement that caused Kay and Rob to jump and it screeched wildly, fighting against the shackles that bound it.

Most of the Serpenduos were aroused by their appearance, making Kay and Rob very nervous as they weaved amongst them. The caged reptiles were covered in golden-brown plumage and the males were adorned with long green feathers, crowning their heads. The females were a little larger and fiercer as they tugged at their shackles. Others were in large cages freely roaming, stalking back and forth. Dandy threw some meat in and they ripped it apart until there was nothing left.

Eventually, they reached a large Serpenduo laying upon fresh giant grass, nesting like a bird. She turned her heads towards them with a stare that warned them not to approach. Dandy, however, crept forward cautiously, entered the cage and left a slab of meat at the side of her nest.

"This is Eve," Dandy told them. "I raised her from when she first hatched. She's always been a feisty one. Now, I must warn you, as soon as Eve starts to lay her eggs, she'll become even more dangerous, so wait outside the cage."

A silence fell upon them as they stared at the creature, all of them waiting. She ate her meat, both heads ripping and shredding savagely. Then she sat back on her nest, as before. It was about five minutes before the creature stirred. She rose to her feet, looking uncomfortable.

The Serpenduo started to act violently. Eve stretched her necks, snapping her jaws at Dandy but didn't leave her nest.

Dandy crouched in the corner of the cage, waiting for nature to take its course. The Serpenduo screeched and squealed inside her nest and then laid her first egg. Dandy quickly snatched the egg and tossed it like a rugby ball down a hatch. The Serpenduo was outraged, shrieking at Dandy, but she remained in her nest as the second egg emerged. Dandy waited, watching the creature carefully. She stared at him in return, her eyes burning and she flexed her tongues, hissing as she licked the air. Dandy knew the creature wouldn't give up her egg so easily this time. He tightened her leash, fixing her heads to the wall with strong vines and then he dived for the egg. The creature tugged and jerked at the vines. She snapped her vicious jaws, trying to attack Dandy, but he got hold of the second egg and dropped it down the hatch. The Serpenduo tore the vines and lunged at Dandy, but he slipped through the cage door and the beast slammed against the bars with utter rage.

"Still one egg to go," Dandy gasped.

Once the Serpenduo had calmed down, she sat back on her nest and when she became uncomfortable again, Dandy slid back into the cage with a different slab of meat. The Serpenduo became excited and snatched at the meat. Something strange had happened though. The Serpenduo was acting like a pet, begging and rolling around in a playful manor to receive this special meat. Dandy refused to give her the meat, but she still begged until she felt her final egg arriving. She laid the egg and guarded it, watching Dandy. Dandy waved the meat around in the air, shielding his nose. The Serpenduo took interest, turning away from her nest. Dandy tossed the meat away from the nest, where Kay heard it squelch as it slapped onto the floor and he waited for Eve to move. The creature stared at the meat and then looked back at her egg.

"Go on, go get your meat," Dandy yelled.

Eve turned her eyes on him, poised to attack and suddenly dashed towards the meat instead and guzzled it down. Dandy snatched the egg from the nest and darted towards the hatch. The Serpenduo finished her meat and ran at Dandy. Kay noticed Alva turn away, frightened for Dandy, and she felt like closing her eyes too, but Dandy responded quickly, pointing his Virga at Eve.

"Perplexa," he yelled and a lightning bolt struck the animal. She stumbled to the floor, looking dazed, and Dandy slid the egg down the hatch and fled the cage.

"Why couldn't you have just... *spelled* it to sleep in the first place?" spluttered Rob, feeling sick from Dandy's near demise.

"Why are you taking away her eggs?" Kay added with concern.

Dandy stood panting, looking bewildered. He muttered, "Humans," under his breath. He then spoke louder, keen to make his point clear.

"Rob, you can't use magic on a pregnant animal; it could affect the infant or kill it. Kay, you need to remove the eggs from a Serpenduo's cage or she will eventually eat her young."

Kay and Rob were a little shocked, but Kay realised a vicious beast like that was likely to eat anything it could sink its fangs into.

Dandy led them to the collecting point of the hatch, and Kay, Alva and Rob took the eggs while Dandy led them through a door into another room. Once they were through the doors, they could hear a chorus of little squeals. Many small Serpenduos were in rows of mini pens, squeaking for Dandy to feed them. Dandy took the eggs and propped them in separate nests.

"It won't take long for them to hatch, and they grow very fast. King Edwin insists I make breeding Serpenduos my specialty; I don't know why, but he seems to want more and more of these dangerous animals," Dandy said, still staring at the three eggs.

"Well, after we snuck into his castle, he probably thinks he's not protected enough," Rob said.

Dandy heaved a sigh.

"I think having Serpenduos running around his garden is mad... remember that piece of meat I held in my hand just now?"

All of them nodded.

"Well, that was Imp meat," Dandy stated and Alva gasped.

"You mean, you actually feed them Nymphas?" Alva cried in protest.

"King Edwin insists on it," Dandy said defensively.

A silence came over them again.

"What's an Imp?" Kay asked.

"It's an imprisoned Nympha," Dandy told her. "They are stripped of all magical ability and their wings and they become pale, crooked creatures," Dandy explained. "They're not considered to be Nymphas any more and no longer have any rights. They're treated worse than any animal."

Kay felt faintly sick by this disturbing revelation.

"Look!" Rob cried.

One of the eggs had begun to shift. They all watched eagerly as part of the shell broke away and a Serpenduo thrust one of its little heads out, the other head slithering out beside it. Its tail was next to thrash out, breaking a hole at the bottom of the egg, crunching the shell into small fragments.

At that moment another of the eggs stirred, toppling over, and the infant inside kicked a scrawny bird foot through the side. Whilst they were all watching this chick, the third chick broke its head through the top of the shell and smashed the rest of its egg with one blow.

"That's a female," Dandy commented.

He approached the little female carefully, sprinkling magic dust around her and her broken egg. The chick rose with her egg, as though she were being lifted in an invisible box, and she was placed in an empty pen. The other two eventually broke away from their eggs, and they were both put in separate cages too.

"Are they dangerous, even as chicks?" Rob asked, noticing the caution that Dandy was taking.

"Yes, they have needle-sharp teeth they'll use on anything, even their own siblings. A Serpenduo has to fight to live from the moment it's hatched; that's why they're so vicious. They hatch quickly and grow up fast, but there are few out in the wild that make it to adulthood. Now that we're breeding them, I suppose that will boost their numbers."

"I don't see why King Edwin cares about the Duo population; I think we should *let* them become extinct," Alva said, looking at the creatures with disgust. "I know that they're good at tracking criminals down and stuff, but now they're starting to hurt innocent Nymphas as well. That's what my mum said."

"Yeah, I agree with you there," Dandy said.

Kay was starting to lose interest in their conversation. She wandered over to the newly-hatched chicks. The female was teaching herself to walk and the other two were wailing and eating the eggs they had hatched from. Kay took the most interest in the female. Her heads were large compared to the rest of her body, which made it hard for her to lift both of them. She managed to stand but tumbled back down again, making a bark-like noise. Undeterred, she tried again, wobbled a bit and then began her first steps, like any newborn.

Dandy joined Kay in watching the young female stalk around her cage.

"C'mon Kay, let's get back upstairs. The chicks need some time to settle."

Kay, Alva, Rob and Dandy all made their way back up to the top of the store on the root.

"We better go now, Dandy. I'm gonna introduce them to some of my other friends," Alva announced.

"Sure, see you around, Alva. Bye, Kay. Bye, Rob," Dandy replied.

"Thanks, Dandy. Bye," Kay, Alva and Rob called in unison.

As they left the store, Alva gave Kay and Rob more of the Silibis petal to eat. They each took three bites and they started to look more like Ever Nymphas. Alva was pleased that they both had yellow hair this time.

"Great, let's go!" Alva chirped, leading the way.

Rob followed him and Kay took one last look at the animals in the shop before catching up with them.

-Chapter 13-
Cosmo and Gem

Alva, Kay and Rob walked a different route back towards the village, looking out towards fields of giant grass blades, swaying in the breeze. They could also see King Edwin's castle towering against the horizon, marking the beginning of a dark and murky swampland. Behind them was a massive expanse of forest.

"The Feature Nymphas live in the centre of Feature Forest, the most dangerous forest in Edenland," Alva said, gesturing to the trees behind them, "and the Floatlies stay in the Floatly Fields, beyond the castle." Alva then pointed to the dark, jagged mountains. "The Onyx Nymphas live over there."

Kay noted the contempt in Alva's voice as he mentioned the Onyx.

"Alva, how far have you been?" Kay asked, in awe of the rolling landscapes around her.

Alva sighed.

"I've only ever been here. That's why I started visiting Earth; I wanted to explore more, but my mum won't let me. Melvin and Merlin get to go places when they're escorting King Edwin. She said I could be a soldier for the king too when I'm older, but I don't want to be a soldier." Alva scowled. "When I grow up, I'm gonna explore all of Edenland and more. I'll travel the entire Nymphas' World and write a book about all my adventures," he said, gazing at the horizon.

They reached Alva's house, went through the bubble and slid down the chute, landing in the hall. Tansy came jumping through to meet them.

"We'd better clean ourselves up in the Dust Room," Alva said.

They all dived into the room, including Tansy, and the blue dust cleaned them up. Once the dust had settled, Kay and Rob noticed with disappointment that the effects of the Silibis had faded and they were back to themselves again. They ventured out into the hall and Jasmine was there. She stood in a handsome dress made from pansies, bright in colour and freshly bloomed.

"Alva, I see you're late back," she said, fixing her hair in a bubble-like mirror.

The bubble dropped and Jasmine stepped over towards them with a beaming smile.

"Mum, you look beautiful," Alva said, smiling back.

"Oh… why thank you, dear. It's the one I made recently," she responded, with a bigger smile. "Now, I must find Kay something to wear. You can find something for Bob. Make sure you hurry though, we don't want to miss anything," she chirped to Alva.

Jasmine took Kay down the root to her own bedroom and showed her a leaf-covered wardrobe containing many flower-made garments, all brightly coloured.

"Ah, here we go, dear; you wear this one. It's a dress I made. I'd hoped for a girl once," Jasmine said, presenting Kay with a white dress covered in snowdrop petals.

"It's gorgeous," Kay squeaked, mesmerised by the dress.

"I'll just change the size, so it fits you," Jasmine added

with a smile and waved her Virga.

"Growig!" she said, and the dress grew to fit Kay.

"Thank you," Kay said appreciatively as she stared at the dress.

Jasmine left the dress on her flower bed and vacated the room, calling, "Don't be long, dear."

Kay lifted the dress; the flowers felt soft and fresh. She took off her clothes and slipped it on with the matching petal shoes. Kay smiled at how well it fitted her. She rushed to the hallway, where everyone else awaited.

Alva was flinging what looked like a dandelion seed and the fluff floated through the air. Tansy jumped up and caught the floating seeds and carried them back to Alva. Rob's jaw dropped when he saw Kay.

"You're wearing a dress!" he exclaimed.

Kay nodded and stared at what the boys were wearing. Alva's garments were like fresh autumn leaves entwined into a formal suit. Rob looked similar, but the colours of his garments were dark blue petals.

"Kay!" Jasmine called, almost in tears. "You suit it so well dear; it brings out the colour in your hair."

"Is that a good thing, you know, since I'm supposed to be a Nympha?"

"Well, I guess the Silibis will take care of that before we go… shame really, it suits that colour more than yellow."

"Okay," Alva piped up, "I've told my friends to come and meet us here," he announced.

Kay wondered what Alva's friends would be like; just like him she supposed. She felt excited that she might be included in a circle of friends and, perhaps, be known as one of Alva's *best* friends.

Eventually, they all heard voices coming from the front door.

"Cosmo, Gem," Alva called as two Nymphas flew into the hallway.

Alva approached a Nympha just a little bigger than himself and hugged him. He then turned to the Nympha who was the height of Kay and gave her an embrace too.

"Kay, Rob, this is Cosmo Pollen and Gem Barley. Cosmo, Gem, this is Kay and Rob... Em, what's your second name?" Alva asked, turning to his Human friends.

"It's Mackenzie," Kay answered, and Alva nodded.

"Cool," Cosmo cried, as he stared at Kay and Rob in wonder. "Real Humans; where'd you get them?" he asked, edging closer.

"They look a little like us," Gem chirped, wandering around them. "Except they don't have wings. They have funny hair too and round ears," she chuckled. "Wow, lots of thumbs!"

"Look, they're not creatures to stare at, okay?" Alva said, standing in front of Kay and Rob.

Cosmo and Gem looked guiltily at their feet.

"Sorry," they said sullenly.

"Okay, let's get going before we miss the first events," Jasmine twittered as she ushered them towards the door.

She passed Kay and Rob a Silibis petal. Kay took three horrible bites and thought only of being an Ever Nympha. Once she opened her eyes, she had curly yellow hair and wings which slipped nicely through the holes in the back of her dress. She also remembered about her hands and was pleased to see two pincer-like thumbs instead of her fingers. Rob did the same and they both looked like genuine Ever Nymphas.

Kay, Alva, Rob, Cosmo, Gem and Jasmine all left the

house on foot, so the Nymphas could walk beside Kay and
Rob. They walked excitedly through the village streets which
were brightly lit by floating oval lights. They then left the
village and headed towards the giant grass blades which were
illuminated by the two moons shining in the night sky. They
trekked through grass to shouts of "Severit" as the Nymphas
used their Virgas to cut a path, but it seemed difficult for them
to find their way as they were so used to flying.

Up above, Kay saw sparkling lights of many colours and
showers of petals floating everywhere, like confetti. Cheerful
music filled the air and shouts of joy echoed amongst the grass.
On and on the Nymphas thrashed until, finally, they reached
their destination: the Ever Celebration.

-Chapter 14-
The Ever Celebration

The tall grass opened onto a large clearing bustling with many Nymphas browsing market stalls loaded with odd trinkets or riding bizarre creatures, screaming with delight. Little stars whizzed around the sky like sparklers and Kay gazed in awe at the beautiful fairy tale scene. Alva looked to his mother excitedly.

"Okay, you can go, but remember to find me when the ceremony begins," Jasmine shouted over the noise.

At those words, Alva grabbed Kay and Rob and dragged them to a stall. Cosmo and Gem found interest in another stall and they parted ways.

"Look, Lazy Shoes!" Alva gasped, pointing at the stall. "*You* could do with a pair of those."

"What do they do?" Rob asked.

"They make you hover, of course," cried the sales Nympha from behind the stall, shaking her head. "What do they teach kids these days?"

"I knew that," Rob said, straightening up, "I just forgot, that's all."

The Nympha stared at him.

"Well, do you want them then?" she asked sternly.

"Yes," Alva replied, stepping in front of Rob, so the Nympha gave Alva the shoes and he handed her some sort of seed out of the silver pouch that appeared around his neck.

Alva walked away from the stall and Kay and Rob followed him to a quiet corner where they wouldn't be seen.

"Go on, Kay, try these on," Alva suggested, handing her the shoes.

The shoes were like transparent rubbery molds of Nympha feet and she squeezed them on. She jumped into the air, expecting to fly off but nothing happened.

"Viva!" Alva said, sprinkling each shoe with Nympha Dust from his wrist. "Now walk, as if climbing stairs and then in a straight line."

Kay lifted her foot and it stopped in midair, as though standing on something solid. She brought her other foot up and then started walking through the air, like there was an invisible floor beneath her.

"Rob, look at me! I'm flying!" Kay squealed with delight, climbing higher and higher.

"Alva, can I have a pair of those?" Rob asked excitedly.

"Yeah, I think we should all have a pair," agreed Alva, and soon they were all in the air.

"You can see everything from here," Kay yelled to her brother as she ran high above the rides and stalls swarming with Nymphas both on the ground and hovering in the air.

"Hey, watch this," Alva shouted, climbing higher by leaping like a frog. Kay copied him, wanting to climb the skies forever.

Alva stopped to admire the view and Kay stood beside him.

"We should probably stop here," Alva gasped, tired from running. "If we go any higher, something might eat us," he chuckled.

Alva, Kay and Rob stood silently as others took to the skies on their wings, and soon the night was glittering with fluttering wings and Nympha Dust. *This is real magic*, Kay thought to herself, gazing for miles all around at the many wonders of Nymphas' World. She felt content in the moment, letting every care simply float away.

They all climbed down from the air and landed in the fairground amongst the rides.

"Let's go on that one," Alva said, pointing to many burrowed holes in the ground, sealed off by a bubble. Kay was about to ask what it was when a large caterpillar-like monster charged from one of the holes and dived down into another at great speed, carrying with it many delighted, screaming Nymphas.

"Wow, a rollercoaster," Kay exclaimed.

"That looks amazing," added Rob.

They joined the queue and Kay's eyes wandered around the other festivities. She saw strange bumblebee creatures flying in circles with Nymphas on their backs clutching their extralong antennae like reins. There were muscular horses with three spiral horns giving rides to young Nymphas and other rides were like dodgems: turtle-like shells protected by blue bubbles which caused them to bounce off one another. There was also an ice rink in the shape of a rolling sea of frozen waves.

Passing by were Ever Nymphas with doughnut-shaped bubbles around their waists. The doughnut bubbles had egg-shaped bubbles circling around them which encased infants. Kay understood these magical rings to be some sort of pram. The Nymphas could walk as they pleased with the babies protected in bubbles swiveling around their waists.

Kay also saw other strange Nymphas. Most had butterfly wings with swirling antennae sprouting from the top of pure white hair. Others had large kingfisher-like wings clad in bright blue feathers and vivid red hair on their heads. Alva noticed Kay staring at the Nymphas.

"They're the Feature Nymphas," Alva called, pointing to the bird-like beings, "and the butterfly Nymphas are the Floatlies."

"Are there any Onyx here?" asked Kay, feeling nervous.

"No," Alva assured her, "they hate Ever Celebrations."

"I'm glad; I don't think I want to meet any Onyx."

Just then, a trumpet fanfare sounded in the distance and Alva gasped.

"We have to go. The ceremony is about to start."

"Awww, I wanna go on the ride," moaned Rob.

"Sorry, Rob, maybe later," Alva said, "after the ceremony."

Kay, Alva and Rob used their Lazy Shoes to climb back into the air and escape the crowds.

"I'm gonna call my mum," Alva told them, rubbing his Tactus. "Hello, Mum, can you hear me?"

"I can!" Jasmine shouted over a noisy crowd of Nymphas.

"Where will we meet you?"

"I'm by the north entrance to the stadium," she informed them.

"Okay, see you there," Alva said and waved for Kay and Rob to follow him.

They all floated down towards a nest formed from living trees, their branches entangled together and beaming with dazzling light. The stadium was constructed from trees, their trunks entangled together to form what looked like a fancy and impressive giant bird's nest.

They found Jasmine, Cosmo and Gem among a sea of Nymphas swarming into tiers of leaves shaped into seats.

"Ah, there you all are," Jasmine called, holding Alva's hand as they joined the swarm.

Alva clasped on to Kay, who clasped on to Rob, and he in turn clasped Gem who pulled Cosmo along with her. Finally, Jasmine found them seats near the back of the stadium. Once they were seated, Jasmine produced a bottle with a glistening spark dancing inside it. She packaged the bottle in liquid gold, flowing from her Virga, and sent it flying through the air to meet with many more golden gifts. They formed a shiny mountain in the middle of the stadium and Kay smiled as the air twinkled with Nympha Dust.

Applause suddenly erupted all around. Alva, Jasmine, Gem and Cosmo stood up and joined in, and Kay and Rob followed suit. An Ever Nympha stood next to the mountain of gifts, and she was smiling gracefully up at them all. She wore a splendid golden dress and looked about the same age as Kay's Granny Isa. She carefully unwrapped her gifts and thanked each Nympha by name. She then fluttered up to a throne of pure gold.

"Hey, look," Rob whispered, pointing to an old Nympha who had entered the stadium.

The old Nympha hobbled out from a bubble-carriage pulled by six silvery-white unicorns and stood smiling with his hands raised, as he too was given thunderous applause. King Edwin wore a suit of bright red poppies with long sleeves that trailed along the ground. Behind him, a regal cloak floated through the air in waves of bright blue silk.

King Edwin flew into the air, his long, thin beard

117

swimming like a tadpole behind him. The crowd applauded again as he landed and a throne magically appeared next to the golden one. He bowed his head to the crowd, his crown twinkling in the floodlights. He stood beside many other Nymphas who had a look of importance. The crowd became silent and King Edwin spoke into a unicorn horn, his voice amplified for all to hear.

"Nymphas of all kinds, we are gathered here to celebrate the Ever Day of Tansy Dock. She has dedicated her life to nursing at Ever Hospital and has helped heal us all from many diseases and injuries. Not only is she a good worker, but she has been a kind friend to us all. She was a devoted sister to her brother, Anther Dock, who, not so long ago, had his own Ever Celebration. Let us all give a cheer for Tansy as she too goes where we have not yet ventured. Now, let the celebrations continue, with one of Tansy's favourite sports. Please welcome the Fable Dancers," Edwin finished, and the whole stadium blacked out as four multi-coloured spotlights shone down on what was now an ice rink in the centre of the stadium, frozen into rolling waves and tunnels.

Five Nymphas dressed in ice-blue costumes skated out into the middle of the rink, and dramatic music began to echo throughout the stadium. The Nymphas glided effortlessly across the ice in expressive dance, mastering the waves with jumps and turns before soaring into the air with flips and spirals. Kay's heart skipped a beat as a bolt of lightning forked through the air, shattering an ice wave. From the debris rose a tempest and an orange light erupted from it as one of the dancers conjured a dragon of fire. Another dancer created a sea serpent of water and the dragon flew at it, slashing its claws while the serpent snapped its watery jaws. Eventually, the serpent's waves of water engulfed the dragon and only smoke could be seen, swirling high up into the air. The dancers were disguised by the smoke and all fell silent. The music faded in again, and out from the smoke floated one dancer, growing shoots of green leaves from her wrists. The other dancers emerged from the smoke and touched their Virgas together, creating a white oval bubble. They ducked back into the smoke and the solo dancer's shoots wrapped around the bubble. The solo dancer then ducked into the smoke too and all that was visible was the bubble, imitating an egg, surrounded by a nest of vegetation perched above the smoke.

After a few moments, the bubble appeared to become solid and the egg cracked down the middle, causing it to break in half. Small flames issued from it, and the egg exploded into a million pieces, all of which disappeared as soon as they reached the audience.

As the debris cleared, a baby dragon of fire came into view. The smoke evaporated and the dragon sank onto the ice, melting a puddle in the centre. The dancers appeared again, one of them controlling the baby dragon as it grew larger and larger.

High above the crowd, a gush of water cascaded in front of the audience. As the water fell, it began to form a creature — the Sea Serpent. The serpent confronted the new dragon as the Nympha dancers controlled it with their Virgas. The dragon fought the sea serpent and defeated it, evaporating its body into steam. The dragon gave a mighty roar of flames and the sound echoed violently off the stadium's walls. Then at once the lights went out, leaving the stadium in complete darkness.

The crowd gave thunderous applause and the lights came

back on as the dancers bowed, skating off the rink. Alva turned to Kay and Rob.

"That's a special dance called the Loom Orbis Dance. The Fable Dancers usually perform it at an Ever Celebration, because it means rebirth. The sea serpent kills the dragon and then, when the dragon is born again, it takes its revenge by defeating the serpent."

"Well done to the Fable Dancers; Miss Dock loves dragons," King Edwin called out of his unicorn trumpet, before passing it to Tansy to say a few words.

Kay saw that there was now a golden cylindrical box in the centre of the stadium floor.

"Thank you all for coming to my Ever Celebration tonight, and thank you, Fable Dancers, for your stunning performance; it's the best I've ever seen," she praised, mopping her tears, and then she took a deep breath. "I've been waiting for this day all my life and…"

Suddenly there was a great screeching cry, and everyone froze as giant bats swooped down from the top of the stadium. At first Kay thought it was part of the ceremony but then all the Nymphas in the stadium began crying out in panic.

One of the bats landed upon the golden box in the centre of the stadium and a tall Nympha, unlike any other Kay had seen, dismounted. He called a spell that blocked each entrance to the stadium to stop anybody from leaving.

Kay turned to Alva and Jasmine, who each had worried faces. Nymphas flew in all directions, desperately trying to escape. Jasmine grabbed Alva and Cosmo, who snatched Gem's hand. Alva latched onto Kay, but Kay missed Rob and he was swallowed up by the swarming crowd. Kay broke away from Alva, reaching for her brother, but it was too late;he was nowhere in sight. The crowd of screaming Nymphas bashed into her and washed her away in another direction. A great booming voice called, "Icen!" and the stampede ceased at once.

Kay found she could no longer push through the crowd, or scream out for Rob. She was frozen still, only able to move her eyes. Kay saw that every Ever Nympha in the stadium had become like a statue, except for the king; he could speak.

King Edwin's voice boomed within the stadium as he addressed the tall, strange Nympha.

"General Douglas Slate, how dare you interrupt an Ever Celebration!"

-Chapter 15-
Over the Mountains

The Nympha glared up at the king, his dark hair shimmering with shades of blue beneath the lights of the stadium. Kay could see his blue-tinged skin and flexing bat wings and realised, with alarm, that he was an Onyx Nympha. There were about twenty of them, their white eyes shining brightly, with no pupils. Each was tall in stature, with talon-like nails on their thumbs and toes. The Nymphas' ears were pointed, resembling a bat's, and each wore animal skins, covering their bodies.

General Slate growled at the king's call and flapped his powerful wings, hoisting himself into the air with one stroke. He landed beside King Edwin, and with a snort he took the unicorn horn from his hand. King Edwin seemed to be frozen up to his neck and could do nothing as General Slate addressed the crowd.

"Fellow Nymphas, I am deeply sorry that we have had to take this action, but it is necessary! You see, among you, there are Humans!" General Slate said, as though Kay and Rob were dangerous animals. "This is why I come into your festival, because you have a traitor among you. Someone is trying to hide the Humans, and they will be dealt with according to Onyx law, unless you own up now and tell me where the Humans are, before I come down and drag them out myself."

As the Onyx Nympha awaited a response from the crowd,

Kay realised she could move her head. She could also talk and wanted to shout to Rob, but she knew that would be risky. There were murmurs from every direction: some called out to find loved ones, while others called for the Humans to be handed over. General Slate glided down to the ground in front of Kay, and her heart pounded against her ribs. He was staring at something and Kay began to panic, feeling certain he was looking right at her. She could feel a scream of fear rising up in her throat but abruptly, General Slate moved on.

"Well, who's hiding the Humans, eh? I'm not going to wait forever. Your time is now, before I let the Barbastelle bats loose," he threatened.

Everyone was silent and Kay felt honoured. All those who knew about her and Rob protected them, although anything could happen.

"Very well then, have it your way," he snapped.

General Slate gave a screeching call and the bats crawled into the crowd. Kay was overcome by fear as the bats sniffed their way around. She gasped as General Slate's bat crawled up to Alva, sniffing at his clothes. It gave a screech and Alva gulped as General Slate approached with a grin.

"Well... how about it, boy; why don't you tell me where the Humans are? You have their scent all over you," he said slowly, interrogating Alva as the crowd looked on.

"Leave him alone," Jasmine cried, but she couldn't help her son. Alva thought fast.

"They're hidden," he said, avoiding the Onyx Nympha's white eyes.

"Hidden..." General Slate began. "Hidden here?" he asked, crouching down to Alva's level.

"No," Alva replied quietly.

"Where, then?" General Slate shouted, violently shaking Alva for answers.

At that moment, a bat crawled up to Kay, snorting and grunting like a pig as it sniffed her clothes. The bat growled at her and Kay felt her heart hammer in panic. Then another bat screamed from the other side of Kay and she gasped as she saw it sniffing at Rob. The bats all crawled over to where Rob was and surrounded him.

"No," Kay called, but none could hear her.

General Slate bounded over to Rob and narrowed his eyes as he stared suspiciously at Rob's Nympha appearance. He withdrew a small pouch from his belt and poured blue dust onto his hand. He blew the dust and it floated through the air, engulfing Rob like a mist. The dust settled and, to Kay's horror, Rob's hair had turned dark and his wings had vanished. General Slate grabbed his hand to reveal four fingers and a thumb; he was now unmistakably Human.

"Take it!" General Slate called to his Onyx guards, and they grabbed Rob, dragging him away. Kay saw a stone drop from one of the guards as they strapped Rob to one of the bats.

General Slate walked back over to Alva with a gloating smile.

"Arrest these two as well," he said, pointing at Alva and Jasmine.

The Onyx closed in, but a dazzling blue light flashed from above and formed a protective bubble around Alva and Jasmine. Kay looked to the sky and saw King Edwin, free from the binding spell, with his Virga aloft.

General Slate growled and a dark blue liquid began spilling from his Virga, forming into a giant sphere around him, the other Onyx Nymphas and their bats. Kay heard Rob calling to her from the sphere and fought with all her might against the spell to go to him, tears swelling in her eyes. She felt her body gradually release as the inky blue sphere sealed and she ran towards Rob, fighting against the stampeding crowd fleeing the stadium.

Kay was close to the sphere and she desperately reached out her hand to Rob.

"Kay!" He screamed from the bat's back, as it leapt off the ground and soared into the midst of the floating bubble that steadily rose out of the stadium. The king shot a web that latched across the top of the open roof, but the bubble broke through and drifted away into the night.

"No, Rob!" Kay called in anguish.

Kay watched helplessly as her brother was taken away, thinking she would never see him again. She fell to her knees, and her tears spilled from her eyes onto a strange-looking stone. Kay realised it was the stone dropped by the Onyx guard and she snatched it up in anger, ready to throw it away, but then she heard voices rising behind her.

"It's another Human," called one of the Nymphas.

"We should hand it over before the Onyx come back," shouted another.

Kay knew they were speaking of her, as she noticed her long red curls dangling around her face instead of the fluffy yellow hair. She suddenly felt numb and didn't notice Alva standing in front of her, trying to talk to her.

"Kay, are you all right?" Alva asked her, looking concerned. "Don't worry, the king will get him back; they'll make a deal. We won't let him get *executed*."

Kay felt a twinge of sickness at that word.

"Executed?" she shouted, tears beginning to fall again.

Everyone stared, but Kay didn't care; her brother was in danger.

"Look, King Edwin will negotiate; he'll bring him back," Alva said, trying to calm her.

Kay didn't know what she should do, so she glumly followed Alva, Jasmine, Cosmo and Gem into the village. Cosmo and Gem went back to their houses and Kay trailed after Jasmine and Alva, clutching the stone she had in her hand as though it were her only connection to Rob.

They reached the green bubble to Alva's house and entered into the hallway. Alva and Jasmine turned to Kay with worried faces, but neither of them seemed able to reassure her. Only *Rob* had that power; he was the one she always looked to for comfort.

"Let's see what the Tactus is saying," suggested Jasmine.

They all wandered through to the sitting room and gazed at the great orange Tactus upon the ceiling.

"Viva," Jasmine announced, pointing her Virga at the Tactus. It revealed a face glaring back at them — General Slate.

Kay felt a shiver race down her spine at this first glance of him. General Slate looked pleased with himself as he addressed his audience.

"At last, Edenland, we have caught the Human. It has been many endless days, but a Human was found endangering the lives of Ever Nymphas during a celebration in the Wood Grass."

The Tactus flashed to an Ever Nympha reporter.

"And now, let's get an insight on what witnesses saw."

The Tactus flashed through a series of Ever Nymphas Kay didn't know.

"Once the Human had been taken, people said there was another one; it had orange hair," said one of the Nymphas.

"There *was* another one, a little girl, I saw her, I was there," said another.

A noise distracted them from the Tactus. Kay, Jasmine and Alva heard someone come down the entrance chute to the house.

"Wait here," Jasmine said, beckoning them to hide.

She held her Virga aloft and tiptoed around the corner, treading as silently as she could.

"Oh, Dandy, it's only you," Jasmine exclaimed from the hallway.

Alva gave a sigh of relief, but Kay was distant. She could only think of her brother. Kay felt a sudden burst of anger and rushed into the hall.

"This is all your fault!" she screamed, pointing her finger at the Nymphas.

The Nymphas looked taken aback and Alva tried to reason with her, but Kay ignored him and continued.

"If we had never gone to that stupid celebration, Rob would be safe, we could have gone home together."

A hot tear started to trickle down her face and Jasmine started to look just as upset. Kay breathed hard now; she wanted to rip something apart. She jumped carelessly onto the root beside her, pushing one of the spots and it shot down, leaving the Nymphas behind.

The root halted at Jasmine's room and Kay rushed in, trying to stop her tears, but it was no use. She screamed and threw away the Onyx stone, hitting the furniture. Kay pulled at the snowdrop dress, but it wouldn't budge. She became aggravated and tore it off, shredding it to pieces, but it didn't make her feel any better. She put on her Human clothes and ran away from the destruction on the floor. Alva and Jasmine were in the hallway.

"I'm so sorry, dear," Jasmine sobbed, trying to embrace her, but Kay ran by and reached for the root.

"Kay!" Alva bellowed, but she wasn't going to stop for anyone; she was going to rescue her brother.

The root took her back up to the hall and Kay ran up it and out of the flower head door. She sobbed the password and rushed out the bubble. It was windy outside and spitting rain, but that didn't concern Kay; she was determined now. She ran through the village and charged into the tall grass. She couldn't see where she was going, but she hacked her way through the green blades, focused on her destination — the mountains, just visible above the grass.

Eventually she could no longer see the mountains, so she slowed to a stop. Kay tried jumping, but it was useless at her height. She thought of Rob, flying on one of the bats, struggling to get away, and she felt her eyes fill with tears.

Kay found the deserted leftovers of the celebration and charged past the horses with three horns, frantic in their field.

"I'll need a fast animal to ride; an animal that can fly," she said to herself, wiping away her tears.

She found what she was looking for: the bees. Kay ran up and mounted one of the bees' backs. It was a calm creature and didn't make any fuss as Kay held its long, rein-like antennae. She didn't know how to fly a giant bee, but she was determined to learn so she could find Rob.

"No!" came a shout, and then she was dragged off the bug. Alva had come to stop her.

Kay tried to regain her breath before speaking.

"I need to find him — tell me where to go?"

"No, Kay, just wait; they can't kill Rob until the Onyx king holds a trial, and that usually takes a week," Alva explained.

"A week..." Kay said, studying the mountain peaks. "Could I get to the Onyx king in a week?"

"You can't go by yourself," Alva begged, grasping Kay's shoulder.

"Alva, I'm getting my brother back, you can't stop me," she said angrily, pushing him away.

"I know," Alva said quietly.

"Then let me go," Kay shouted at him, trying to mount the giant bee again.

"You can't fly, Kay."

"Why not?" Kay growled, sliding back off the creature.

"Because, the Onyx will expect that."

"I don't care; I'm going to get Rob and..."

"Then I'm coming with you," Alva interrupted.

"What?" Kay said.

"We're friends, Kay; I'm coming with you. I don't know what's out there, but what I *do* know is that the Onyx patrol the air, especially at night."

"So, you're going to help me get Rob back?" Kay said with surprise.

"Of course," Alva replied. "Friends help one another and we're not going to let Rob die."

Kay grasped Alva into a hug. She was going to get her brother and go back home.

"Let's go," Kay announced, feeling more assured.

"Not yet, we need to convince my mum that you believe King Edwin will get him back. Then, when we go to bed tonight, we'll meet up at... midnight," Alva proposed. Kay was about to protest, but Alva hushed her. "That way, I can somehow tell my mum what we're doing in a note and we can get away in time so they can't catch up," he explained, and Kay nodded in agreement. "We'll take the Mini-ponies and... the seeds," Alva said, holding out his silver pouch that formed from his skin. "Oh, and this!" he added, taking out a stone from his pocket. It was the stone that Kay had thrown away in Jasmine's room. Alva gave her the stone and she studied it.

It was a black stone, perfectly round, gleaming and shiny. The middle of the stone was a lighter shade of grey. It was a perfect oval shape and protruding from one end of the stone was a black curled vine which was shaped into a 'T'. Kay stared at it for a few seconds and then glanced at Alva.

"Alva... Ah!" she screamed, as the centre stone turned into a white Onyx eye and she dropped it. "What *is* that thing?" she squeaked, trying not to scream again as the white eye rolled around in its stone socket.

"It's a key!" Alva told her.

"One of the Onyx dropped it," Kay recalled.

"It might be a key for the castle," Alva said. "We're lucky you picked it up; it could come in handy," he praised as Dandy approached.

"Quick, hide it!" Alva warned Kay, and she stuffed the stone into her pocket as Dandy raced over to them.

"What do you two think you're doing?"

"Nothing, Dandy. We're coming home," Alva piped up, and he nodded to Kay. Kay nodded back in agreement to the plan they had made and followed Dandy back to Alva's house.

Dandy repeated words like "irresponsible" and "dangerous" to Kay and Alva, but being told off didn't displease Kay now that she and Alva had a plan to set things right. When they entered the house, Jasmine was whispering to Melvin and Merlin, who had just returned from Evertrunk Castle to give an update on Rob.

"King Edwin says that the Onyx are ignoring his pleas," stated Melvin to the household, "and they're going ahead with the execution. Apparently, King Natale has given his brother permission, but we all know better. The prince will be keen to get the job done himself."

They quickly stopped talking when they noticed Kay, and Jasmine gave her a sympathetic smile.

"I think it's about time you two were in bed," she suggested, eyeing the root.

"C'mon, Kay," Alva whispered gently, grasping the root and taking the journey to his bedroom.

Kay peered around at the hall of Nymphas, still feeling angry. She knew now though that she wasn't angry with them any more; she was angry with herself. She should have never agreed to go to the Ever Celebration.

"Don't worry, we'll get your brother back," Melvin tried to reassure her.

She sadly mounted the root and vanished down the dark chasm. She dashed into her earthy-smelling room and climbed into her bed. She lay there, feeling the stone in her pocket as she waited, impatient to use it. Time was going slow; *too* slow.

-Chapter 16-
Evertrunk Garden

It was ten o'clock and Kay was still wide awake, watching the glowing bug next to her bed. It was trying in vain to escape its cage and Kay kept picturing Rob in a cold, damp prison cell, whilst she lay cosy in a bed.

She watched the bug until midnight approached. She had ten more minutes until she was to meet Alva. Kay got out of bed and prepared herself for a long and perilous journey. Five minutes... four... three... two... one. Kay crept out of the bedroom door and silently tiptoed towards the root. She pressed the brown spot and it took her down to the Mini-ponies' level. Kay was full of anticipation as the root came to a halt. Alva was already there, stuffing a few items into a large silver pouch. He looked up at her and smiled with evident excitement.

"I have Loom Stones, my Mist, Ever-Aquati, Ever Biscuits, magic seeds, Flam Oil..." Alva said, restraining his voice to a whisper. He placed each item in the pouch as he announced it, "My Catalop's ear," he said, attaching the ear to his belt. "Oh, yeah, and I have my Virga, a map of Edenland and the *Book of All*," he added.

"The *Book of All*?" Kay repeated.

"The *Book of All*'s a book written by the Mother of All. *She's* the only one who's ever seen all of Nymphas' World.

This book can help us if we don't understand some of the advanced magic we might face on our journey."

The book was bound in an ancient leather-like material, with a miniature portal on the front cover that swirled with vibrant colours. Alva placed it in his pouch.

"All set," he announced, letting the large pouch sink into his skin and disappear.

He gave a soft whistle and the stable doors swung open. Two ponies trotted up to meet Alva, and he used his Virga to lift two leaf-saddles into the air and prop them onto the ponies. Alva helped Kay up on the copper pony.

"This is Fidus which means 'trusty', and my Mini is called Fulgur which means 'lightening'," Alva said with a smile.

He mounted his silvery pony and pointed his Virga to the far side of the stables.

"Aparta," he called.

The earth trembled and parted. Alva turned his head to Kay and she glared ahead. The ponies waited patiently for the word.

"Kay," Alva whispered, "this is it; there's no turning back."

Kay felt a little hesitant, but this was her decision; she must find Rob.

"Let's go!" she said.

"Canter," Alva ordered and the Mini-ponies shot off through the gap in the earth.

Once on ground level, Alva closed the earth behind them and they sped through the protective bubble of the house and out into the village. It was still spitting rain outside and Kay pulled up her hood, tightening it against the cold, blustery wind. She noticed Alva was wearing a cloak of a shiny blue leaf-like material, and he drew up his hood too, inspecting the map as the ponies trotted out of the quiet, still village.

"Okay," Alva began, "we'll need to cross Evertrunk Gardens to reach the swamp."

"Swamp! But I thought we were going to the mountains?" Kay asked.

"Yeah, but to get to the Onyx Mountains we'll need to go through Dreepy Swamp; it'll be safer trekking through the castle grounds than meeting a quick end in the grass! We should have brought the Lazy Shoes," Alva said, rubbing his forehead in frustration.

Both ponies entered into the woods, passing the familiar strawberry school and eventually approaching the grass blades that encircled the castle grounds. Alva pointed his Virga.

"Who goes there?" commanded one of the blades, but it was too late.

"Severit," Alva yelled and a red firework shot from his Virga.

The grass blades screamed as the spell cut them down to the ground.

"Alva, that was horrible," Kay whimpered.

"Oh, don't worry, they'll grow back," Alva assured her.

He peered around the grounds, looking out for guards on Serpenduos. One was heading their way, so Alva steered Fulgur behind some bushes and Kay followed, hiding the ponies in the dense foliage. The Catalop's ear started to twitch and Alva touched it to hold it still.

"If we're caught, those Serpenduos will kill our ponies," Alva fretted, calming Fulgur by stroking his nose.

Kay did the same to Fidus as the Serpenduo slinked closer with its heads bobbing. It sniffed around for intruders and hissed every so often, its tongues flicking in and out. Alva tried to move Fulgur, but the pony wouldn't budge. It stood, shocked and frozen by the Serpenduo's appearance.

Alva gritted his teeth as the Serpenduo snooped around the hiding spot. He readied his Virga, looking afraid, and Kay held her breath. Alva slid silently off his pony and signalled for Kay to do the same. She did so just as the Serpenduo stuck its head through the bushes. Alva pulled Kay to the ground and smacked the ponies on their hind legs, causing them to dart away. The Serpenduo snapped at them and the guard lost control of the reptile as it lunged after the Mini-ponies, chasing them out of the grounds.

"C'mon, this way," Alva squeaked, nudging Kay to follow.

"What about Fidus and Fulgur?" Kay whined, unable to see whether the ponies were safe.

"Don't worry, they can outrun a Duo. We'll meet them at the other side," Alva whispered, pulling Kay across to a giant flower bed.

They pushed through the large flowers, and the Catalop's ear wriggled again as another guard and Serpenduo came close, but they passed by without a glance in their direction. Alva breathed heavily, trembling as they passed. His behaviour was making Kay slightly nervous too. Alva gave the signal that the way was clear and Kay emerged to a view of the barn where the unicorns were kept. Kay realised it was open ground for many metres around them and feared they would be exposed.

"Let's head to the barn for cover," Kay said, and Alva nodded in agreement.

They dashed towards the barn, but halfway across the

clearing, Kay saw the Catalop's ear twitching again and heard the murmur of nearby voices.

"We're not going to make it," Kay gasped with a surge of panic.

"Yes, we are," exclaimed Alva, grabbing Kay around the waist and launching them into the air.

For a brief moment, Kay glided through the air, breathless at the sensation, before crashing to the ground with a thump inside the barn. Alva lay beside her, panting, whilst the unicorns became restless at their presence. They had pearl-white coats that seemed to glow in the darkness. They were more slender than the horses Kay had seen on Earth, and their spiral horns glistened like crystals upon their heads. The unicorns shied away into the darkness at the sight of them and Kay and Alva heard other voices approach the barn.

Two guards appeared at the entrance with orb-like torches, and Kay and Alva shuffled into a corner, out of sight.

"Do you really think Humans are dangerous?" asked a young Nympha with a moustache, glancing around the barn.

"Well, I think they could be dangerous... yes, I mean, you've heard the way they destroy their land and wage war on one another constantly," answered the older Nympha through a bushy beard.

"But surely we could take on Humans; we have magic."

"Yes, but you can't be too cautious, son. Humans are extremely powerful; it's best we have nothing to do with them," finished the older Nympha.

The guards moved on and Alva waited a few moments before signaling for Kay to follow him. He latched onto Kay and flew with all his might over the rest of the clearing and into a cluster of trees. No more guards were in sight, so they passed through the wooded area and into another part of the royal garden containing exotic plants and large ponds.

Kay noticed that the rain had stopped and the wind had eased. The clouds had disappeared and everything seemed clear again.

"How long will it take us to get over the mountains?" she asked.

"It should take us about three days; that's what Merlin said when he escorted the king there," Alva said.

Kay felt relieved to hear this and was hopeful they'd get there in time.

Alva ran across the garden and Kay followed behind, dodging ponds and dashing across bridges made of vines and tree trunks.

Kay and Alva saw an old giant tortoise lumbering around a grass patch and it grunted, eyeing them with suspicion. The Catalop's ear twitched in its presence.

"We'd better get out of here before it tells King Edwin," Alva fretted, heading swiftly onwards.

Kay saw a necklace around its neck and thought it must be treated like royalty too. She turned away and followed Alva over to a large gaping pond.

"This pond carries all the way across the garden," Alva said, his eyes following the pond's calm surface.

"Right, so what's the problem? You can just carry me across, right?" Kay replied.

"No, I can't, there's a protective barrier that I can't fly through," Alva said, trying to fly at the pond and bouncing off the invisible barrier.

Kay studied the air and Alva looked at her with concern.

"So, what are we going to do?" she asked, looking back

the way they'd come.

"We can't swim or I'll lose my dust and won't be able to protect us." Alva frowned.

"If we have to swim then so be it," Kay said exasperatedly.

"Wait, I'll check the *Book of All*," Alva said.

The large silver pouch appeared around his neck and he rummaged inside it. He brought out the book and stuck his hand into the miniature portal on its front cover. Kay watched as the book jumped off his hand and slammed onto the ground. It began flipping through its pages, stopping at "Enchanted Concealments". The pages were inscribed in an ancient language with diagrams that moved. The portal resided on every page and an image like a hologram popped up from it — the Mother of All. She looked like her statue, with an air of wisdom. Her hair hung like dull, yellow string and her clothes were that of royalty. She was smiling and glancing around her, finding both Kay and Alva.

"You have reached the chapter of Enchanted Concealments, my child; what do you wish to know?"

"I wish to know... em... how to go through an Enchanted Concealment," Alva said.

"Does the Enchanted Concealment have a password?" the Mother of All enquired.

"I don't know," Alva murmured, staring at the lake of water ahead.

The figure in the book turned to the pond and smiled.

"Ah, one of the enchantments I placed myself!" the Mother of All announced, nodding reassuringly.

"So, you know how to get by it?" Alva asked, a smile now appearing on his face. The Mother of All smiled back at him.

"Yes, but what is your purpose in getting through?"

"We need to save my friend's brother; he's in danger," Alva replied bravely.

The figure considered them both for a moment.

"Indeed, then I must tell you how to get by. This enchantment holds no password, but there are words that will help you summon a plant of great use to you."

Alva nodded, encouraging her to carry on.

"They are called Risus Lilies. To call upon them, announce 'Risa-bobbin' and the plant's lily pads will rise to take you across. To cover your path, just enunciate 'Sinkisub', and the pads will sink back into the pond," the figure finished.

"Thank you," Alva grinned and the book banged shut.

Suddenly, Serpenduo screeches rang out all around them, and Kay and Alva knew the guards were coming closer.

-Chapter 17-
The Verli

Alva stood at the water's edge and called, "Risa-bobbin!"

Seconds later, something moved silently below the water. Bubbles began to erupt to the surface and Kay looked behind, seeing the guards, approach nearer. The lily pads emerged from the water, their leaves like stepping stones across the length of the pond. Kay touched the first pad with the tip of her shoe and recoiled in fright as it giggled.

"The Risus Lilies; of course, Laughing Lilies," Alva recalled.

The guards were drawing ever nearer so Kay took a deep breath and stepped onto the pad, ignoring the plant's giggles. It was extremely unsteady, and she thought that at any moment she'd be in the pond. Striding to the next pad helped her balance.

"Te-he, ha-ha, he-te-he," sounded the plant's giggle, as if being tickled.

Kay leapt like a frog from one lily pad to the next and Alva followed behind her, the plants becoming hysterical with laughter. Another shriek echoed through the darkness and the Catalop's ear wriggled furiously; Kay and Alva knew they had been spotted. The guards rushed towards them, casting spells through the air, but they all bounced off the enchantment.

Kay reached the other side and cried out, "Hurry, Alva!"

Alva picked up his pace as the guards charged across the lily pads in pursuit, shouting angrily. Alva dived off the last pad onto the ground, pointed his Virga and yelled with gasping breath, "Sin... ki... sub!"

At once, the lily pads sank beneath the surface and the guards splashed into the water. Kay grabbed Alva and they ran through the trees, desperate to escape, whilst the guards bobbed up and down in the murky water, furiously gargling insults. They ran and ran, their faces flushed red, until they reached a vine-covered wall. Alva grabbed Kay and tried to fly over it, but it was no use; the garden was full of Enchanted Concealments, preventing him from ascending into the air. He brought out the *Book of All* again.

"No," Kay shouted, "we don't have time for that!"

Alva slipped the book back into his silver pouch and studied the wall. He tried to fly again, but his wings stiffened under the power of the enchantment. He wiped his brow and grasped the plant that clung to the wall, heaving himself up in an effort to climb it. Kay started climbing too but soon noticed that the vines were moving.

"Alva," Kay said in a concerned voice, "what *is* this?"

"I don't know, you wouldn't let me check," Alva shouted back from above.

"Well, it's moving," Kay said, latching on tighter to the vines.

Alva wailed above her. A vine had grabbed him off the wall and hoisted him into the air.

"Alva!" Kay cried.

Kay tried to jump off the wall, but she was snatched as well.

"Severit!" Alva yelled, swinging his Virga wildly.

The plant's vines severed as though cut with an invisible knife, and Alva was dropped on the other side of the wall. The plant gave a shriek of pain and the vines unwound to reveal cat-like eyes and a ferocious mouth at its centre. The plant eyed Kay cruelly, coiling another few vines around her as it raised Kay high above the wall, squeezing her neck and chest. Kay wheezed as the vines tightened and tried desperately to wriggle free.

"Vivagon!"

Kay dropped to the ground outside the castle gardens as the plant shrank down behind the wall, wailing at the loss of its vines. She caught her breath, gasping for air, and turned her head up to see Alva hovering high above her in a dazzling glow. He slowly lowered himself to the ground and crouched down beside Kay.

"That was a Sherba," Alva told her, evidently pleased with his rescue.

He held the *Book of All* in his hand at the chapter headed "Carnivorous Plants".

They heard voices coming from over the other side of the wall; the guards had managed to catch up with them.

"Did you see where the intruders went?" asked a voice with authority.

"No, sir, they must have gone over the wall, sir," replied another Nympha.

"Well, search the perimeter and send scouts to look around the swamp."

Kay and Alva gazed at what lay before them. It was a sorrowful jungle of weeping trees and plants continuing on into the swamp.

"We've got to go now, before they catch us," Alva told

Kay, sounding anxious.

He quickly made a cricket sound into the night and Fidus and Fulgur trotted out of the woods. Kay smiled at being reunited with Jasmine's faithful Mini-pony, but her heart gave a lurch as she realised Fidus had a gash on the side of her hind leg. Alva saw it too.

"She wasn't fast enough for the Serpenduo," he said, inspecting the slash.

"Will she die?" Kay asked sadly.

"Maybe, but there's no time to help her now," Alva said with haste. "Get on her; we need to get going!"

Kay scrambled upon Fidus and called, "Canter," and the Mini-pony bounded into the swamp. Alva called out as well and Fulgur galloped behind her.

The swamp was damp and eerie as they followed a path through slimy vine-covered trees. On either side of them were murky ponds bubbling with foul-smelling odors and a thick sludge on the ground that was hard for the horses to trot through. The two moons were the only light to guide them, but as the jungle thickened that light soon faded. No animals called into the night and the Catalop's ear was frozen still. Yet, Kay had the impression that they were no safer in this place than in the castle gardens. Ever had seemed cheery and magical, but *here,* Kay could only think of all things dark and miserable. Thoughts of Rob, alone and afraid plagued her mind. The dampened feelings also extended to her mother, in floods of tears for her lost children.

Alva hopped off Fulgur, summoning his silver pouch. He rummaged in the bag and brought out an oval stone. He tapped his Virga on it three times and the stone lit up. He rummaged in his bag again and brought out a bottle of ointment. He squelched through the mud to Fidus and dribbled some of the ointment onto the pony's wound, causing it to seal into a scab. Fidus neighed with relief and Fulgur trudged over to Alva, rubbing his head against Alva's back in gratitude.

"It's not safe here, we have to keep moving," Alva said to Kay, looking around at the dreary swamp.

Kay gave a nod and pulled herself up on Fidus again. Alva fluttered up onto Fulgur and they both called, "Canter" at the same time. The Mini-ponies raced through the mud, sending wet dirt flying in all directions as they ventured farther into the swamp.

*

Much time had passed since Kay and Alva had stormed into Dreepy Swamp. Alva ran his thumbs down the map, working out where they were.

"We're just a little behind schedule," Alva told her.

The ponies were tired and so was Kay and even Alva dropped his eyelids every now and then. The ponies trotted at a slow pace and Alva peered around every tree for danger. He took deep breaths whenever the ponies swiveled their ears around, listening for anything alarming.

Alva urged Fulgur forwards, giving him a nudge at his neck. The beast had wide eyes and kept his distance from the trees and water, only daring to tread on the scarce path. Kay felt afraid too. It was extremely dark, and she was using a Loom Stone to reveal any hidden dangers, but the faces of the weeping trees and the wind rustling their leaves played upon her mind.

The path became narrower and muddier, hindering the

progress of the ponies. Even with the stone lights it was hard to see a clear path ahead of them through the dense foliage.

Gradually, the thick swamp trees started to thin, letting the sky and moons peek through again. The pale light shone upon the stagnant pools and Alva halted, spotting bubbles fizzing on their surfaces, accompanied by strange gurgling noises. Alva gulped and Kay gave a shudder that caused her teeth to chatter. Alva glanced between the frothing pools, accusing each of having life hidden beneath it. The Catalop's ear was also twitching, causing Kay and Alva to become very nervous.

Alva raised his Virga as they hesitantly shuffled by the gurgling pools. Fulgur and Fidus were extremely difficult to guide, jumping at the slightest movement upon the wind. The path became narrower and narrower still, the dark water creeping up to meet them. Fulgur and Fidus grunted each time the cold, murky water lapped against their hooves. Alva gave a gasp.

"Verli!" he cried, pointing to what looked like a bobbing piece of seaweed emerging from the pond. "Strak!" he called out.

"Alva?" Kay cried, as a flash of light cut through the gloom and into the water, causing a tremendous splash.

The creature was too fast though; Kay shone her stone at the pond and saw the creature duck to avoid the spell. The water became still again, and Kay and Alva held firm on their ponies, with bated breath. Fulgur began rocking, frantic at the Verlus' appearance.

"Let's get out of here," Alva yelled to Kay and screamed, "Canter!"

Fulgur charged through the shallows, soaking Fidus and Kay and causing Fidus to lurch backwards in panic.

"Canter!" Kay spluttered, choking on the water, but as Fidus tried to move, she was tugged back.

Her hind legs seemed to have sunk into the mud and her back end was slipping towards the revolting pool behind her. Kay's heart leaped frantically against her ribcage as she saw a slimy green frog-like hand holding firmly onto Fidus' tail. Kay screamed and Alva heard her from up ahead. He doubled back to help as Kay stared in horror at the grotesque head of a Verlus surfacing from the water.

Red unblinking eyes peered out from behind long seaweed-like hair hanging over its face. Muddy saliva frothed from its mouth behind the seaweed as it hissed and gurgled aggressively at Kay. Another dark webbed hand latched onto the pony's tail and Fidus' hind legs sank below the water, drawing Kay nearer to the creature's grasp. It reached for Kay, suddenly jumping out from the water to reveal a muddy body, and a slimy fish tail that looked more like a frog's leg.

Kay screamed out to Alva again as the Verlus' wet hand slithered around her arm and dragged her under the water. Kay fought for breath, thrashing against the Verlus' grip, but its other webbed hand clasped her face in a powerful hold. The creature's swirling seaweed hair revealed its face and Kay could not help but stare into the void of the Verlus' mouth, gaping across much of its face. It had no teeth but bared its gums menacingly as it tried to drown her.

Kay saw a spell swim through the water towards the Verlus, but it quickly fled from it, like a darting fish. Kay seized the opportunity to swim for the surface, but the Verlus quickly grabbed hold of her foot and tried to drag her down again. Kay stamped her free foot down upon the creature's head with all her might until it released her with a growl.

Kay reached the surface to find many Verli closing in. Alva shot another spell at the creatures, and this time he was successful, shrinking one of them to the size of a tadpole. All the other Verli scattered, and Kay clambered out of the pool, coughing up its murky contents.

Fidus was struggling to get out of the mud while Fulgur danced in circles with worry. Kay and Alva ran to Fidus' aid, pulling at her mane and eventually hoisted her out of the mud.

At the same time the Verli were gathering again, their seaweed heads bobbing in the water. Alva jumped back onto Fulgur and Kay, soaking and damp, climbed back on Fidus, who was now sticky and muddy. Panic overcame the ponies and they raced through the flooded path but were halted abruptly by a tremendous splash.

A Verlus had leaped out of the water and gripped around Fulgur's hind legs. The pony kicked the Verlus off and it squealed, wriggling back for the water. Alva raised his Virga but realised it was soaking wet and would not work, so quickly summoned the silver pouch and snatched out a bag of seeds.

A Verlus sprung upon Kay and Fidus from behind and grabbed Fidus' tail again. It lashed out for Kay and Fidus kicked her hind legs, just missing the creature. The Verlus pulled harder on the tail, reaching for Kay again but missed and fell to the ground. Alva threw one of the seeds at the creature.

"Tendrila!" he cried and vines sprouted out of the seed, wrapping around the Verlus and sending it crashing back into the pond.

More Verli came bounding out of the water towards Kay and Alva.

"Save the seeds and run!" Kay bellowed to Alva, and they

hastily rode away, the ponies galloping in full stride. They were racing so fast that when Kay heard a cry in front of her, she couldn't stop Fidus and they went hurtling down into an enormous ditch. Kay, Alva, Fidus and Fulgur were now trapped.

-Chapter 18-
Aylwyn

Kay's body ached all over and mud and slime covered her clothes and skin. She opened her eyes to find her waist drowning in mud and beside her was Fidus, trying her best to keep her head above the surface of the sludge. Fulgur seemed to be unconscious and Kay couldn't see Alva.

"Alva, where are you?" Kay frantically called to the mud, wondering if he had gone under.

"Kay?" came a squeak, struggling to be heard.

Fulgur awakened and scrambled up. Underneath Fulgur was Alva, caked in mud.

"Are you okay?" Kay asked anxiously and Alva nodded, trying to catch his breath.

They looked around and found no way to escape the ditch.

"Help! Can anyone hear me?" Kay screamed through tears.

Alva tried to climb the muddy walls but just slipped down again. He gave his wings a go, but they were covered in mud, too sticky to fly.

Kay called desperately to the world above; she didn't care who heard her now. Their need was dire and she even hoped for some of the Ever guards to come and take them to safety. Rob was so far away, too far away, and Kay was trapped, unable to escape. She began to cry, the tears spilling from her eyes, feeling she had failed Rob, condemning him to his fate.

Alva patted her on the back.

"Don't worry, Kay; we'll get out of here," he said, trying to comfort her.

Alva wiped the mud off his hands and summoned his silver pouch, which appeared around his neck. He felt inside and withdrew the *Book of All*. He stuck his hand in the portal and the book jumped off his hand and fell in the mud.

"Great," Alva huffed.

The book had gone under, and Alva rummaged around in the sludge, trying to find it.

Kay heard gurgling noises from above and looked up to see three seaweed heads peering down at them.

The gurgling changed, sounding like malicious laughter as Alva frantically searched for the *Book of All*. He finally hauled it out of the mud and held it up against the wall, as he thrust his hand through the portal. The pages moved but were soaked and the Mother of All flickered and then vanished, causing the light of the portal to fade as well. Alva looked crestfallen, as though that was their last hope. He placed the book back in his silver pouch and sank back into the mud in defeat.

The Verli still lurked above, waiting for them to die, and Kay ran at the muddy walls that imprisoned them in a desperate effort to escape. She dug her hands and feet into the walls, trying to climb, but the mud simply gave way and she slid down.

"Help!" Kay called out, but the Verli only growled back, as though her call were a threat.

Kay and Alva then heard a squeak and a growl, a great wail and then a crunch.

"Something scared the Verli away," Alva whispered, sounding afraid.

He backed up to the muddy wall and Kay followed suit, hoping for whatever it was to pass by.

"Hello," called a squeaky voice, "who's there?"

It was a quiet, soft voice and Kay gave a look to Alva, but he still seemed petrified.

"It's coming closer," he whispered.

Kay could hear it coming closer too; perhaps it could help them?

"We're down here," Kay called, wading into the centre of the ditch and waving her hands.

Alva ran out too.

"What are you doing!" he snapped. A creature peered over the top of the ditch. It had a pointy snout and large front teeth. Its whiskers twitched around the edge of the hole as its pink nose sniffed the air. Its paws had stubby pink fingers with white claws, and Kay could see glimpses of its brown coat. It caught sight of Kay, Alva and the two ponies.

"You see what you've done? It sees us now... it's... it's... it's a Quatmus!" Alva said in surprise.

"A Quatmus... is it a friendly creature?" Kay asked.

Kay could now see that it was a massive mouse head that was staring down at them with four eyes. It twitched its whiskers some more and moved its large ears to catch what they were saying.

"No, they're not and it can't help us anyway," Alva told her.

"You don't know that," argued Kay.

"It's no use Kay, you can't talk to mammals!" Alva moaned at her.

"Excuse me, can you help us?" Kay asked the Quatmus, undeterred.

The Quatmus caught sight of Kay and replied, "Yes... I think I can help you."

Kay grinned at Alva. "Thank you."

Alva gave a look of disbelief. The Quatmus turned away and dropped its long tail down the ditch.

"Grab on!" it hollered.

Kay caught hold of the mouse's tail and used it as a rope to climb out of the ditch.

She could now see the Quatmus closely. It was the size of a fully grown lion and had four black beady eyes, shining in the moonlight. The beast had two front paws like any other mouse but four hind legs.

"Shall we get your friend out then?" it asked.

"Yes, please," Kay answered, and the beast tossed its tail down the hole again.

Alva reached for the tail and began to climb. The Quatmus dug its claws into the ground and gave uncomfortable squeaks as Alva slipped on the muddy wall. Once he was up, he still looked puzzled.

"So, wait a minute," he puffed, "you can talk to that Quatmus?"

"Yup," Kay replied with pride.

"Then you must have the Gift of Speech," Alva said, sounding impressed.

"Em... hello?" the Quatmus called impatiently.

"Oh, right, my name's Kay," she announced, extending a hand to the Quatmus. The Quatmus looked a little confused by this gesture but raised a paw. Kay took his paw and shook it. The Quatmus quickly withdrew and stood back.

"Honoured to meet you, Kay, my name is Aylwyn," the Quatmus replied with a bow. "You're a Human," he said, curiously, "I remember you. I saw you near the waterfall in Ever."

Kay thought back. She hadn't met him at the *falls*; she had been with Rob. Then it dawned on her.

"You were the animal in the woods, when I was chasing that bug," Kay recalled. The Quatmus nodded and looked around at the ditch where the poor Mini-ponies were still stuck.

"Can't you get Fidus and Fulgur out?" Kay pleaded.

"Sorry, but I think they'd be a little *too* heavy for my tail," Aylwyn replied, shaking his head.

"What are we going to do? We can't get the ponies out!" Kay moaned to Alva.

He stared at the ditch with a sigh.

"We'll need to leave them," Alva said sadly. "We can only hope other Nymphas find and rescue them," he said. "We need to get going, but..." he paused, searching his belt, "The map, it's gone," he squealed.

"How are we going to find our way now?" Kay whined, but Aylwyn heard her.

"Where are you going?" he asked.

"We need to get over the Onyx Mountains. We need to find my brother before he's executed," Kay said breathlessly.

"Luckily, you've found a Quatmus who knows the swamps, forests and mountains, as they are my home," Aylwyn said, with a nod and bow.

"What are we going to do?" Alva asked, still staring at the ditch.

"You really can't hear Aylwyn, can you?" Kay asked with

a grin.

"Who's Aylwyn?" Alva asked in confusion.

Kay laughed.

"C'mon, Alva, Aylwyn knows the way. He's gonna take us to Rob!" Kay squealed with delight.

*

The swamp began to get lighter. The sun was rising in front of them, and all the plants, trees and ponds came into focus. Gradually the birds arrived and sang from above and the animals approached the swamp. Kay saw that the path became drier, and the mountain peaks came into view. The Onyx Mountains spanned across the horizon, their faces of dark rock cast in ominous shadow. She felt anxious as she gazed at them, so Kay watched the large Quatmus in front of her instead, as he guided them along the forking paths. Alva didn't seem to trust Aylwyn. All night he had complained about how the Quatmus would lead them astray. Kay was glad that Alva and Aylwyn couldn't understand each other or Aylwyn would surely be offended. Kay had grown so tired of Alva's attitude towards Quatmi that she'd started to trek beside the beast and allow Alva to whine behind her.

"So, Aylwyn, how long is it until we reach the mountains?" Kay asked conversationally.

"Soon, I expect," replied the Quatmus. "I think it's near my nap time though," he added, trundling on.

"Aylwyn says that we'll reach the mountains soon," Kay shouted back to Alva, who still seemed to be moaning.

"How long is *soon*?" Alva asked irritably.

"Aylwyn, how long is *soon*?" Kay relayed.

At once, the Quatmus stopped in his tracks and sat upright. Aylwyn pointed with his paw to the left of them.

"You see that large black twiggy bush?" he said. "That's where the swamp ends and where we can rest."

Kay gave a sigh of relief as the rotten vegetation and stagnant ponds gave way to thriving green plants and trees. The canopy of trees receded to reveal the mountains close at hand, dominating their view. Kay stared at the sheer faces and rocky peaks towering high above and felt very nervous as she wondered how they would climb over them.

They reached the bush and Aylwyn ripped off some massive leaves to make himself a bed. Kay and Alva followed suit, collecting a smaller pile of leaves for themselves. Aylwyn then curled up, tucking each of his six feet under his fur and closed his four eyes. Kay gently snuggled up beside Aylwyn, resting her head on his furry back. The Quatmus did not protest but welcomed her, twitching his whiskers as she got comfortable. Alva, on the other hand, tried to create a bed like his own back home but failed miserably without his Virga working. He threw the leaves on the ground in exasperation and lay down, crossing his arms in protest at how close Kay was getting to Aylwyn.

Kay continued to gaze at the dark mountains looming menacingly above them, stealing all the light from the world. She could see the beginning of the endless and terrifying path hewn from its rugged face and felt a shiver of apprehension at the prospect of what lay ahead.

*

It was mid-afternoon when Kay awoke. She realised Aylwyn wasn't beside her as she felt her head against the leaves. Kay looked over to Alva, but he was still asleep, so she got to her feet and explored her surroundings.

The sun was high in the sky and life filled the forest in every sight and sound. A harmony had settled in the atmosphere, and Kay almost forgot the nightmares of the swamp. She heard a strange chomping sound behind her and jumped as an animal raced up to her. She relaxed again when she realised it was Aylwyn. He was carrying what appeared to be a limp young deer in his jaws which he dropped at Kay's feet.

"You should eat this to keep your strength up, Kay," the great Quatmus suggested, offering her the dead animal.

Kay noticed Alva was awake now.

"Alva, will we eat?" Kay piped up, noticing how dull his skin had become without his magical Nympha Dust.

"No, we're not eating *that*; I've got some food for us in my pouch," Alva said, reaching into the silver pouch that appeared from his skin.

Alva brought out red biscuits from a cocoon. He passed one to Kay, but she didn't feel like a biscuit. She was extremely hungry and wanted something more substantial. However, she didn't want to fight with Alva so she ate it. The biscuit was dry and boring, but Kay felt like she could eat no more. Alva then passed her a beautiful silver flask carved with flowery decorations and precious stones, and Kay drank from it, slurping down the Ever-Aquati. With just one sip her thirst was gone.

Kay watched Aylwyn rip into his prey. It was amazing to see this Quatmus eat like a tiger, when the mice back on Earth were small vermin. Alva was making cringing faces as Aylwyn ate his meat.

"What's wrong with you?" Kay muttered.

"He's eating a Catalop calf," Alva said in disgust.

Kay turned to Aylwyn.

"Why are you eating a baby one?"

"Well, they're easier for a six-legged Quatmus like me to catch and this one was sick, so I put an end to its misery," Aylwyn replied between mouthfuls of raw meat.

Kay beckoned Alva to come closer, but he crossed his arms and refused to go anywhere near the Quatmus. After Aylwyn had eaten, he settled down on the bed of leaves again.

"So, what were you doing in the swamp last night?" Kay asked Aylwyn.

"I was hunting; I'm nocturnal and I usually like a Verlus for my dinner," Aylwyn told her, showing off his sharp teeth at the thought of such a meal.

Kay grinned, as it looked as though Aylwyn was smiling. Kay liked Aylwyn and she was glad he was helping her.

A half hour of rest went by and then Aylwyn announced that they should be on their way. He headed towards a series of caves that lined the base of the mountains.

"Where's he going? Ater is that way," Alva said, pointing to the path.

"Aylwyn, why aren't we taking the path?" Kay quizzed him.

"The path is used by many Onyx Nymphas and curious travelers. I presumed you'd wish to avoid them so we're going a route that will take us up to the heights of the mountains, away from prying eyes," he explained.

"Yeah, that's a good idea," Kay agreed and told Alva, who

stood defiantly with his arms crossed again.

"It looks dangerous," Alva protested.

"But Aylwyn says that this way is faster and the Onyx don't go this way," Kay argued, and Alva stared at the caves. "We need to get to Rob as fast as we can, Alva. Please, let's go this way," Kay pleaded.

"Okay," he sighed, and they followed Aylwyn towards the caves.

-Chapter 19-
The Caves

Kay and Alva climbed up into the caves after Aylwyn. The Quatmus scurried up with ease and entered into a dark crevice. Kay entered the darkness, placing her feet as carefully as she could on the uneven surfaces. She bent her ankles awkwardly many times as she tried to keep pace with Aylwyn. Alva was worse; he was used to flying instead of climbing, and his pincer-like thumbs on his hands and feet made it very difficult for him to balance on the rocky terrain.

Aylwyn continued to lead them through the maze of caves, squeezing and crawling between cramped spaces.

"Aylwyn, how much longer do you think we'll be in the caves?" Kay asked, feeling nervous in the dark enclosed space.

"We're almost there, just one more," Aylwyn told her, and Kay felt a hint of excitement; they were getting closer to Rob.

Aylwyn went through a small gap in the rocks. It was so small that Kay had to crawl into it. She didn't like this at all. Kay could just spot the tip of Aylwyn's tail in front of her. Behind her she saw Alva's worried face.

"We can't go through *there*!" he protested.

Kay continued on.

"It gets wider!" she called back to Alva, and she heard him start the tunnel, muttering.

Kay kept her eyes on Aylwyn's tail, and she began to see

more of him as the cave got larger and lighter. *The end*, Kay thought desperately.

Aylwyn scuttled out of the tunnel and Kay rushed to join him. The sunlight was blinding after the darkness of the caves, but soon she saw the black, colossal peaks before her. Alva joined them and he too stared at the formidable Onyx Mountains.

"I never thought they'd be this big," Kay said.

"They're a lot bigger close up. I've never climbed a mountain before," Alva told her timidly, and she clasped his hand.

"I've never climbed one either, only hills. Just stick close to me and I'll help you," Kay told him confidently, and they started on the steep, rocky path together.

On and on they trekked amongst the sharp black rocks that seemed to scowl at them with their cragged faces. Even the vegetation looked charred, but despite this, animals were all around, feeding off the coal-coloured trees and bushes. An ash-like substance floated in the air, and as it drifted by, Kay realised it was clusters of wind-dispersed seeds. She watched them glide off the mountains, staring into the vast distance she and Alva had covered, Evertrunk Castle now just a speck on the horizon.

A thick canopy of clouds bore down upon them as they neared the top of the first peak. The path was becoming steeper and the strain of pulling Alva up was tiring to Kay's weary body, but they staggered on together, eventually reaching the summit.

It was a brilliant feeling to have finally reached the top, but as Kay looked onwards, there were so many more peaks still to climb. She dropped to the ground in despair and gasped out a few words to Aylwyn.

"How many more mountains do we have to cross?"

"We have two more mountains to climb, but don't worry, the mountains from now on will be a lot less steep. I think we should reach Ater in about three days," Aylwyn told her. "But right now, let's get dinner."

Aylwyn ran away with his nose to the ground, and Kay turned to Alva, who was waving his sparkling Virga around.

"It's working again," he called out excitedly. "This'll make dinner a bit easier."

Kay grinned. She guessed that Alva had become sick of the biscuits too and wanted something different to eat.

At that moment, Aylwyn came scurrying back with an animal in his mouth, dropping it at Kay's feet. It was like a donkey with long rabbit ears and insectile wings.

"A Catalop," Alva said, recognising the animal.

Alva wandered over and ripped off some meat with a knife from his Virga.

"Kay, can you get some sticks?" Alva asked, and Kay collected all she could find in a pile.

"Flam," Alva called, and flames shot up from the wood.

He cooked the meat over the fire whilst Aylwyn devoured the rest of the Catalop. Then Kay and Alva ate in silence, staring at the mountains ahead, wondering what creatures might be lurking amongst the rocks.

After they had eaten, Kay and Alva explored the mountain top. There was a small spring, flowing with fresh water. Although it was quite chilly, Kay and Alva washed themselves, removing the mud from their skin and clothes. Alva used a spell to dry Kay and himself, and then they sat next to the fire and rested a little, before Alva took the *Book of All* to the spring and wiped it clean. He handed it to Kay whilst he settled himself next to the fire again and practised using his Virga on the flames, making them dance and swirl. Aylwyn was cleaning himself with his tongue, licking off all the dirt of the day.

Kay stuck her hand into the portal of the *Book of All* and it jumped away from her, flipping open to the contents page. Kay noticed that there was a chapter on Humans and felt compelled to read it, so she closed the book and inserted her hand into the portal again. This time, she thought very hard on the word "Humans", and the book leapt from her hands once more. The pages flapped onwards until an image of a Human appeared, moving across the page. It looked lifelike as it stared up at her, and then the Mother of All emerged from the portal.

"What is it you wish to know about Humans, my child?"

"Oh!" Kay flushed. "Erm… I don't know," she finished, slamming the book shut rudely.

Talking to a book was a bit awkward for her. *I think I'll let Alva do the reading in future*, she thought, handing it back to Alva.

"Kay," Alva piped up, "there's something I want to look for up here, something that might help us when we go into Ater Castle," he explained as they both stood up.

"What are we looking for?" Kay asked him.

"It's called a Silver Twigged Tree and it produces a substance called Snow Cream," he told her.

"What does it look like?"

"It's a sparkly silver colour and its stems twirl up. They usually grow in clusters upon the mountains," Alva explained.

Kay and Alva searched for the Silver Twigged Trees, leaving Aylwyn sleeping by the fire. They searched behind every bush and in each crevice out to the east side of the mountain. They then scoured all the way around to its north face and to the west, until they found themselves upon the ridge of the south face.

"Look!" Kay called, pointing to a row of nests perched on the edge of a cliff.

She tiptoed towards them and saw what looked like brightly coloured green rocks inside. Alva shuffled by her.

"Rupe-gull eggs!" he squeaked delightedly and began collecting some. "They're still fresh! We can eat them for breakfast tomorrow."

Kay helped Alva gather the eggs, crouching down near the cliff edge. As she did so, she saw something twinkle on the side of the mountain. She looked closer, realising it was Silver Twigged Trees, sparkling in the fading light.

"Alva, there they are!" Kay shouted to him.

Alva quickly put the eggs into his silver pouch, and they crept along the cliff until they found a path of stepping stones down to the Silver Twigged Trees.

Alva snapped off as many twigs as he could carry and so did Kay. They bound them up into bundles and Alva used his Virga to shrink them, before placing them into his pouch.

They headed back up the mountain and found Aylwyn in the same spot. The sky was turning very dark now, so they extinguished the fire and settled down for the night. Kay rested against Aylwyn's soft fur and so did Alva this time. This made Kay smile; Alva was now warming to Aylwyn. They felt exhausted after their day of hiking, so they shut their eyes and easily fell asleep.

*

Kay, Alva and Aylwyn woke up as soon as the sun began to rise, but Kay still felt exhausted from yesterday. Aylwyn caught himself some breakfast, a young Catalop again, and Kay and Alva fried the eggs they had gathered the day before. Kay found that she enjoyed her fried eggs, which was strange because she usually disliked eggs. The egg yolk was actually sweet, like custard. Once they had all eaten, they set off over the next mountain.

As Aylwyn had said, the path was much easier to walk along. Descending the mountain they had climbed, wasn't steep, as it led straight on to the next mountain. The peaks soon rose above them again and they stopped for a quick rest, as Kay was getting blisters from her trainers. Alva's feet, however, were worse, continually bleeding. Alva was able to heal his feet with the Flam Oil he had brought, but he didn't want to use up too much; he feared they may need it again during their journey. A little drop of the oil was able to apply fresh skin to Kay and Alva's blisters, and after a short break they carried on, following Aylwyn into the mountain crevasses.

*

All day long they walked, wary of the mountains' wildlife and treacherous terrain. It was mid-afternoon and Kay didn't feel like they were getting anywhere because after every peak they climbed, another part of the mountain showed itself. By the end of the day, they were staggering and stumbling over the rough ground, feeling fatigued. All that kept Kay going was the thought of seeing her brother again.

"The Onyx Mountains have seventy-seven peaks all together," Aylwyn explained as they hiked. "They surround Ater and reach all the way to Crystallo of the North. There are three major peaks between Ever and Ater: we've already climbed the smallest of those peaks, called Mount Primon, and this one is called Mount Intentus. The last is called Mount Tremor and is the largest and highest of all the Onyx Mountains. Ater sits on the top of the next mountain, Mount Formid," Aylwyn told them.

They each turned the bend and the tallest of all the mountains looked down upon them, its face dark and devious. It was a mountain that struck fear into Kay.

"That, my friend, will be the hardest for us to conquer," Aylwyn told them, wandering on.

Kay scowled at the mountain. She was sure she could make out menacing eyes, furrowed brows and a grin of sharp stone teeth upon it, but her train of thought was suddenly interrupted by a great screech from the clouded sky above. Alva darted into the nearest bushes to take cover. Aylwyn ran behind large rocks and Kay ducked, hoping that she hadn't been spotted.

The creatures were the Barbastelle bats and they descended low, on the lookout for intruders. All the animals bounded away, frightened by the bats. Kay leapt towards Alva and stumbled behind the bushes beside him.

Another screech sounded as the bats hovered above Kay and Alva's hiding place. The wind was blowing strong and their thin membrane wings flapped like kites, billowing in the wind. One bat swooped down to meet the glistening onyx rock of the mountain and began sniffing around, its pig-like nose detecting even the slightest scent. Its ears were twice the size of its head, so it could hear a heartbeat like a drum. It was close to Aylwyn, and the other landed nearer to Kay and Alva. The first bat screeched in anger and Kay realised that she could understand them.

"How dare you!" it squealed, and the other bat crawled over beside it.

They had found Aylwyn and he had scratched the bat's snuffling nose.

"Ha! A Quatmus! Get it!" the other bat shrieked.

The noise was too much for Alva to handle; he clasped his hands on his ears as the two bats attacked Aylwyn.

-Chapter 20-
The Black Gate

Kay started running towards the bats, but Alva pulled her back.

"We have to help him," Kay cried.

"No, Kay," Alva whispered, "we won't be able to rescue your brother if we get ourselves imprisoned." He quickly looked around. "This way."

Alva hid behind every bush as he got closer to the commotion and Kay followed, wincing at every attack on her friend. When they got as close as they could, Alva poked his Virga through a bush and whispered, "Slumbus," causing the beasts to drop limply to the ground.

Kay ran over to Aylwyn and panicked, as she saw how badly wounded he was. Alva quickly brought out his Flam Oil and began dripping it onto a deep gash across Aylwyn's back. The Quatmus grimaced as the magic liquid seeped into his flesh. It created a scab that sealed the wound, and Aylwyn stood up with no pain or discomfort. Kay smiled, and Aylwyn too seemed pleased with his remarkable recovery.

"Tell him, thank you," the Quatmus said, looking appreciatively at Alva.

Kay's smile widened.

"Aylwyn says, thank you," she told Alva.

"Tell him, it's my honour," Alva replied respectfully as he too smiled at Aylwyn.

Kay did so, and then she peered down at the bats in disgust, remembering the ones that had sniffed out her brother and flown him to prison.

"Did you kill them?" she asked Alva, but he shook his head.

"No, they're just asleep," Alva said, "so we better get out of here before they wake up."

Kay, Alva and Aylwyn continued on, a little shaken and edgy as they watched the skies and around every corner. Nightfall came sooner than Kay expected, so she, Alva and Aylwyn made camp at the bottom of Mount Intentus. The travelers enjoyed some dinner caught by Aylwyn and tried to get some rest.

Kay tossed and turned uncomfortably, as she felt something hard in her pocket. She took out the item and remembered: the Onyx key. Its eye was closed so she stared at it in fascination.

"That key will come in handy," Alva told her sleepily. "We can use it to get in the castle."

"Do you really think this key belongs to the castle?" Kay asked him.

"Yes. It looks similar to the keys that Melvin and Merlin carry for Evertrunk Castle. Theirs are made of bark, but they're the same shape and they all have the vines," Alva informed her, pointing to the T-shaped plant growing out of the stone. "That part unlocks the door."

Kay didn't think the stone looked anything like a key, but she trusted Alva. She slipped the key back into her pocket and snuggled up to Aylwyn. Alva huddled into Aylwyn too, and they both fell asleep.

*

Kay awoke in the middle of the night. She wandered away from Aylwyn's squeaky breathing and Alva's snoring and set off to be alone. Kay was worried about Rob, and she felt time slipping away. Her thoughts raced with panic and doubt:

Maybe the Onyx Nymphas hate Humans so much they'll skip Rob's trial and kill him straight away? I might not get to him in time, but I need to try; life without Rob would be unthinkable.

Kay began to sob, the tears spilling from her eyes. *Oh, why did we ever leave home? Rob wouldn't be in this mess if I hadn't followed Alva,* Kay thought bitterly, crying long into the night.

*

Early next morning, Kay found herself in the same spot. Alva had woken her, worried after realising she had strayed from the camp. Alva saw her tear-stained eyes, and there was an unspoken understanding. They ate breakfast in a subdued silence before setting off up the slopes of Mount Tremor.

The mountain was steep and unfriendly, which made Kay and Alva lack the faith to keep on going. The view of bats flying overhead was becoming more frequent and they were losing more and more time hiding from them. Still, they kept on walking, because Rob's life depended on it, but their exhaustion and lack of food was taking its toll. Aylwyn tried to drive them forward, but the wind was searing in Kay's ears, causing agonising aches. *Keep on moving, just one foot in front of the other*, she told herself encouragingly.

*

Kay watched the sun sink into a bath of orange clouds whilst she, Alva and Aylwyn set up camp for the evening. The moons were gazing down on them from the sky as they lit a new camp fire upon the mountain. Kay flopped down beside the crackling fire, feeling drained of all energy. Her eyes settled upon the red moon high above. As she watched it, the red moon slowly aligned in front of the larger white moon, looking down on Kay like a large eye. Kay had always found Earth's moon rather creepy. Her mother had told her that the moon was the protector in the night, but Kay couldn't trust its glowering face.

Aylwyn gave a deep sigh; his nocturnal instincts were keeping him awake. Kay could tell he disliked being awake during the day, but he never complained, which made Kay feel bad each time she fussed about *her* tired body. She had also noticed that Alva had removed his Tactus ring, wanting to avoid any contact with his family. She knew it must have been difficult for him to leave them behind for her.

Kay's gaze was suddenly attracted to the mountainside by a distant light. It was moving rapidly, bounding off the rocks and approaching closer. Kay jolted upright, taking her eyes off the entity for only a second to alert Alva and Aylwyn. All three were seized by fear as the entity halted in front of their camp. The light dimmed slightly to reveal a massive lion head, shaking its mane as it growled. It gave a mighty roar and planted two front paws firmly on the ground, as though preparing to pounce. Kay, Alva and Aylwyn shouted out in panic, but their cries were interrupted by angry hissing and bleating from behind the lion head. The creature turned and Kay saw a goat's rear and hind legs, with a goat's head in the centre of its back, flopping from side to side. The beast flicked its tail aggressively, and Kay noticed that it was, in fact, a snake's body and head, slithering in the air.

"A Chimera!" Aylwyn gasped, cowering before the great beast.

A gust of fire exploded from the lion's mouth, angered that Aylwyn dared speak in front of it.

"You cannot pass over this mountain. Leave or we shall devour you," the lion bellowed with another roar of authority.

"I'm sorry!" Kay piped up. "But, you see, I need to get to Ater to save my…"

"Silence!" the lion cried, interrupting Kay.

"Do you understand him?" Alva whispered to Kay.

"Yes," Kay whispered to him, "we're not allowed to pass."

"Chimera are guardians of the mountains. I've heard tales of travelers who have bargained with them for passage. Ask it if we can make a deal, you know, bribe it to let us pass," Alva whispered back nervously.

"Hurry now, we're starting to get hungry," the lion head growled, and the goat head sniggered excitedly.

"What if we gave you one of our possessions?" Kay began.

"No!" came the lion's loud voice, enraged by Kay's offer, but then the snake tail hissed into the lion's ear and the lion paused in thought.

"What sort of possession?" the lion asked, considering Kay's offer.

Kay looked past the lion's head and stared at the serpent.

It moved closer, eyeing her eagerly.

"Give me the silver pouch, Alva, they're going to take something," Kay told him, and Alva passed it to her without hesitation.

"Come now, tell me what you will give us?" said the lion impatiently.

"I want, I want!" snapped the goat, its head still flopping from side to side.

"Quiet!" snarled the lion to the goat.

Kay pulled out the first object that came to hand, avoiding the *Book of All* and the Flam Oil. It was the cocoon that held the biscuits inside. She opened it by dragging her fingers along the seal.

"Food!" cried the goat, who was easily pleased.

"You'll need to do better than that!" growled the lion, releasing another roaring flame.

At that moment, something else dropped out of the cocoon, and Alva swooped down and grabbed it.

"What's that?" demanded the lion.

"Is it more food?" called the goat.

"They want to know what you've got in your hands," Kay said to Alva.

"It's a Mist," Alva said, turning his back on them, and Kay told the Chimera.

"Mist!" yelled the lion. "We already have mist in the mountains," it said, giving another roar of flame.

Kay's heart was pounding against her chest. She frantically rummaged in the sack and found the Loom Stones that they had used in the swamp.

"What about some Loom Stones?" Kay suggested in a wavering voice, holding up one of the oval-shaped stones and giving it a tap to ignite it.

At once, all three of the beast's heads were amazed.

"A pretty light!" squealed the goat, and the lion looked delighted at such an object, but the snake hissed in his ear again.

"Be quiet, serpent!" snarled the lion. "We'll take the stone," said the great cat, and the goat bleated with delight, but the serpent wasn't convinced. It hissed some more, looking dissatisfied.

"A Loom Stone has other properties that may come in handy," the lion replied to the serpent as the Chimera leapt down from its rock and landed in front of Kay.

The serpent wrapped its slim body around each of the stones and lifted them to the goat's head, which took a few in its mouth. Then the creature bounded off in a blaze of light, into the darkness.

Kay felt as though she could breathe again and Alva and Aylwyn gave sighs of relief.

Kay and Alva snuggled into Aylwyn again as he lay down to sleep, but they each found themselves peering wide-eyed into the night.

"Alva, what was that thing that you rescued from the Chimera?" Kay quizzed him.

"It's a Mist; a means of communication. I thought it would be good to have on our journey. If you get into trouble and can't move, you can use your Mist in an emergency... Watch this," Alva said.

He released the Mist from its smaller cocooned tub. Sure enough, a small cloud of mist hovered into the air before Alva. It was like a cloud, and Alva breathed it in and the Mist disappeared for a second, then he breathed it back out. The

Mist zoomed over to Kay in a flash, waiting in front of her.

"Breathe it in," Alva told her.

Kay breathed it in. It wasn't like normal mist at all; there was something strange about it. Kay heard a voice in her head.

"Kay, can we go to sleep now?" the voice echoed. It was Alva's voice.

She breathed it back out and it floated back to Alva, who put it away.

"Cool," Kay said, and Alva faced the other way to go to sleep.

"Goodnight," he whispered.

"Goodnight," Kay said back, and then she drifted off to sleep.

*

The next morning, they set off, following a ridge rising high onto the daunting peaks of Mount Tremor. All day long they climbed steep rock, carefully edging around thin ledges with sheer drops. Kay felt it was best not to look down, and Alva used his wings to fly if he fell. It was certainly different terrain; even Aylwyn slipped several times. Kay had to take breaks as she became out of breath, and just as she felt she could go no further Aylwyn cried out, pointing in the distance. She looked up and spotted it; the summit revealed itself from behind the clouds.

They reached the summit by early evening. Kay was weary and sore, but began to feel hopeful, as she stood at the end of the mountains.

Kay, Alva and Aylwyn marched down Mount Tremor with renewed vigor and determination. They followed a narrow, winding path that led them to an onyx stone staircase. Alva was able to fly again, his wings now fully recovered, so he flew down to where the stairs were, keeping low so nobody would see him.

It was nightfall by the time they reached the bottom of the mountain. Before them was a massive black wall. In the middle of the wall was a large iron gate, barring the way into Ater. Alva flew along the wall and found that there was no other way in. He tried to fly over, but there was a powerful Enchanted Concealment barring the way so that he couldn't pass. The only way in was through the Black Gate.

-Chapter 21-
The Tree of Knowledge

Darkness had fallen and the sky was like black silk sprinkled with twinkling stars. Kay, Alva and Aylwyn stared at the Black Gate which was at least forty metres high and designed as two black trees entangled together. It had many small gaps so they could see the landscape of the castle grounds and the castle itself; a dark, tall building on a hilltop that Kay thought looked like black upside-down icicles.

Across the gate were words of the Old Nympha language, which Alva could read fluently.

"Ater Gate will yield to none but the Onyx Nympha," he said aloud.

"So, we can't get in?" Kay uttered with despair.

"Don't worry, Kay, we'll find a way in," Alva told her.

"Do you know how to get past the gate, Aylwyn?" Kay asked, turning to the Quatmus, but he shook his head.

"I'm sorry, but no Quatmus has ever been able to get through *this* gate. Even the Onyx Nymphas rarely use it. They usually fly above the gate," Aylwyn added.

Kay growled and kicked the stubborn gate.

"Look, the *Book of All* got us past the Enchanted Concealment in Evertrunk Castle, so maybe it has the answer," Alva suggested, bringing out the old book and sticking his fist through the portal.

The book jumped away, flipped its pages to the chapter of Enchanted Concealments and then the Mother of All appeared.

"How can we get past an enchanted gate?" Alva asked the Mother of All, and she turned to view the colossal gate.

"Does the gate have words, my child?"

"Yes," Alva replied and told the words of warning to the Mother of All.

"Well, this Enchanted Concealment wasn't made by me, so I can only suggest that an Onyx trait will let you pass by," the book advised.

"What do you mean?" Kay said, shaking the gate in exasperation.

"The Onyx have designed this gate so no other race of Nympha can trespass; only an attribute the *Onyx* have will let you through."

"Great, so we have to be *mean* or *power hungry* or — wait a second — how about *killers*?" Alva suggested with sarcasm.

"I'm sorry," replied the book. "That is the only way you can pass through," she finished, and the book slammed shut.

"Alva, you know more about the Onyx than I do, so what can they do that you can't?" Kay quizzed him.

Alva pondered, gritting his teeth and muttering to himself.

At that moment, a cry echoed loudly in the sky.

"The bats," Alva wailed, and they all ran for cover.

Kay watched as three bats glided through the Enchanted Concealment, each shrieking in unison as they approached.

"That's it!" Alva whispered excitedly, looking at Kay.

Kay nodded, understanding his meaning. She knew exactly what she had to do.

Kay, Alva and Aylwyn crept out from their hiding place and ran back over to the gate.

"Go on, Kay," Alva encouraged.

Kay stepped in front of the gate and tried to find the bats' noise inside herself. No one spoke as she took a deep breath and let out a high-pitched screech. Alva had to cover his ears and Aylwyn cringed at the noise. Once Kay felt she had made the horrible noise for long enough she stopped, but nothing happened.

"Was that not it?" Kay asked, sounding disappointed.

"No, Kay, that was it," Alva reassured her, rubbing his ears to recover from the noise.

"That was perfect, completely amazing!" Aylwyn told her, in awe.

All of a sudden, the gate began to creak. The two black trees started to untangle their branches and slowly separate, groaning from the strain of moving.

At last, the gate scraped to a halt, leaving a gaping entrance for them. Beyond the gate they saw a garden that stretched all the way up to the castle.

Alva joined Kay, looking in awe but also deadly afraid. He studied their surroundings. To the right of the garden stood tall, drooping trees with swirled trunks of metallic copper. To the left were murky ponds, lit by glowing bugs in cages. In front of them was a lane, leading towards rows of dark hedges enclosing areas of deep blue grass. There were also clusters of lofty plants on an island surrounded by water which Kay recognised as Silibis.

Kay glanced at Alva beside her but noticed that Aylwyn had not joined them at the gate.

"What's wrong, Aylwyn?" Kay asked, concerned.

"I'm sorry, Kay, but I can't go in there," Aylwyn replied.

"Why not?" Kay asked, surprised.

"You only asked me to take you *over* the Onyx Mountains, and now that you know *where* to go, you don't need me any more," the Quatmus claimed.

"What's up with Aylwyn?" Alva enquired.

"He's not coming with us… I only asked him to take us over the mountains," Kay said sadly.

"Well, that's *typical*," Alva growled. "I knew he'd ditch us as soon as he could."

"Why can't you come with us to the castle? What if we need you?" Kay pleaded.

"I'm sorry, but I have other things to attend to," the Quatmus told her, and, with those last words he scuttled off back up the stairs of the mountain.

Kay had felt much safer with Aylwyn around, and watching him leave brought back all the fear and doubt from the first night when they were trapped in the pit. She had also come to consider Aylwyn a friend and felt abandoned by the Quatmus.

"C'mon, Kay, we don't need him," Alva assured her, taking a step forth into the garden.

Kay still watched Aylwyn climb the mountain terrain as the Black Gate began to move. She quickly ran over beside Alva as the gates clanged shut, trapping them inside the garden. Kay and Alva scanned the grounds for any danger and then began to walk through the garden, keeping off the main pathways.

Kay's palms were sweating and her heart pounded violently as she drew closer to the imposing castle. She realised that she had *no* plan and pondered, anxiously, on what they were about to attempt.

"Alva, what exactly is the plan?" Kay asked, trying to sound as calm as possible.

"The plan is that we put on the Snow Cream and use the Onyx key to get into the castle. It'll be swarming with bats and Onyx guards inside and there might be other dangers that we don't know of. If we fail, the Onyx will kill us *and* Rob without trial," Alva concluded, looking sadly at Kay.

Kay stopped in her tracks and slumped to the ground, overwhelmed by fear. Entering the castle could mean their death and Rob's doom.

Alva knelt down beside Kay, meeting her eyes with a sympathetic gaze.

"Sorry, Kay, I shouldn't have said that."

"No, you're right. You shouldn't have come with me. We could be making things worse," Kay worried.

"Look, Kay, we've come this far, to give up now would be a waste," Alva told her. "We *can't* stop! *We'll* get Rob and bring him home and then you can return to Earth and be with *all* of your family."

Kay sat silently, staring at the murky surroundings. She knew Alva was right, but her confidence had failed her. She imagined Rob in a cold, damp dungeon awaiting execution and their mother crying, all alone. She pictured the sneering Onyx and felt a sudden surge of anger that brought her to her feet.

"You're right. This is all because of *them*," Kay cried defiantly. "Rob doesn't deserve this. We have to save him."

Alva took Kay's hand and nodded. Kay smiled softly at him, appreciating that Alva had stuck by her every step of the way.

Kay and Alva strode forward with renewed confidence, stepping onto a bridge of sparkling black stones. As they crossed, they heard a loud buzzing noise approaching. Suddenly, large insects swarmed around them. They were reminiscent of large flying ants, with tails of blazing flame, like the creature that had lit her room in Alva's house.

"Flintly Bugs!" Alva wailed as the insects began to attack, painfully searing their skin.

Kay tried to whack and kick them away, but the insects just attacked again. Kay and Alva were forced to run, and they both leapt off the bridge, Alva taking to the air and Kay falling onto the embankment by the water. Alva flew for the trees and Kay ran for the path, but the bugs followed close behind. Kay charged along the path into a cluster of withered trees and glimpsed a shimmer of light as a familiar feeling of stretchy plastic brushed her skin and engulfed her.

Kay found herself inside a metallic grey bubble which repelled the pursuing bugs, bouncing them away into the distance. Kay wondered how she had got through without a password but was relieved to escape the Flintly Bugs. She gingerly touched her throbbing neck and cheeks, but no serious harm was done.

Once the Flintly Bugs dispersed, Kay looked around the bubble and noticed a large black tree standing in the centre. The tree was in a cage that surrounded its trunk, but the branches had slipped through the bars, offering an inviting bounty of luscious dangling fruit.

Kay wandered over to the trapped tree, intrigued by its appearance. It had a strange face that was one minute old and wizened and the next young and smooth, fading from one into the other, over and over. Its expression changed as well, transforming between mischievous and fearful. It cradled one of its fruits close to its trunk and heaved in breaths, as though it were afraid of Kay. Kay felt just as afraid of *it*, but her curiosity took over.

"Hi…" she began as she approached it cautiously. The tree gave a gasp as she spoke. "What type of tree are you?" Kay asked it.

"A *good* tree, a *good* tree, I really am!" it said breathlessly.

"Okay, calm down. I just wanted to know what fruit you're holding?" Kay added.

"*Good* fruit, very good fruit," it told her.

Kay was beginning to regret this encounter already.

"It is unusual to see a Human here in Edenland again," the tree croaked in a sly voice.

Kay didn't really want to talk to the tree any more and looked to the castle. She made to turn, but the tree squealed, "Wait, please don't leave, come and stay for a while."

"I'm sorry but I can't stay; I need to find my brother."

The tree began to act peculiarly. Its face molded, forming into a familiar face — her *mother*.

Kay gasped.

"I'm leaving now," she warned the tree, feeling uneasy.

"Kay, is that you?" cried the face.

It *was* her mother's voice.

"Mum?" Kay wailed, running up to the tree.

"Kay, where are you?" her mother responded. "I've been trying to find you. Come home, Kay, please." Her mother paused for a moment and looked terrified. "Where's Rob? Is he there with you?"

Before Kay could answer, her mother's face disappeared from the tree and it reverted to its own, still flickering in age and expression.

"I see your mother is sad, *very* sad," whined the strange

tree.

"Let me speak to her. I need to tell her about Rob and where I am. Please, just let me speak to her," Kay pleaded to the tree.

"Yes, yes, of course, but there is *another* way," the tree said in its croaky, sly voice, its eyes widening excitedly.

It extended a branched arm, revealing the fruit within its twigged fingers. The fruit glowed in the shade of the bubble and Kay's eyes were transfixed by its ruby-red sheen.

"An *apple*?" Kay questioned. "How can *that* help me?"

"No, no, child, don't be foolish, this is no *common* fruit that I hold - it has *many* powers," the tree uttered seductively. "This is the key, the key to transport *you* to *her.* Just one bite and you'll be safe with your mother again; your brother too, unharmed," the tree finished, waving the fruit to and fro.

This was exactly what Kay wanted. She knew it was strange for the tree to know such things, but she didn't care; she just wanted to go home with Rob.

"Just one bite?" Kay questioned again.

"Yes, child, just *one*," the tree hissed.

Kay reached out for the fruit.

"No, Kay!" bellowed a voice from behind.

Kay spun around and saw that Alva had entered the bubble.

"Don't be fooled by the tree, it's caged for a reason."

The tree gave another hiss to drown out Alva's voice.

"No! He's the foolish one; he leads you to your doom. The fruit, child... The fruit — it will take you and your brother home and solve all your problems," the tree ranted. "This one, his plans won't work, and you'll fail and your brother will *die*," it barked.

Kay looked towards Alva again, panicked and confused.

"Don't listen to it. It's all a trick. Taking a bite of that fruit will have severe consequences."

"No, no, I'm a *good* tree, I'm only trying to help," it squealed.

"Shut up!" Alva yelled. "You're an *evil* tree and you should have been chopped down long ago."

The tree cringed and whimpered.

"C'mon, Kay, let's go," Alva told her, grasping her arm tightly.

Alva used his Virga to force his way through the strange bubble and pulled Kay with him, back to the lane.

"I'm sorry, I just thought if there was an *easier* way," Kay said, avoiding Alva's eyes.

"Kay, *many* have been tricked by the Tree of Knowledge. It has a knack for persuading those it encounters to eat its cursed fruit; that's why it's caged and shut away in that bubble. I'm just glad you listened to me," he smiled.

"But I was so stupid, I shouldn't have let it try to persuade me," Kay moaned, disappointed with herself.

"Kay, if it had shown *my* mum, asking *me* to come home, I would have eaten the fruit in an instant," he said with a grin. "Luckily, I know about the Tree of Knowledge and its tricks. Now, let's find your brother," Alva told her as they continued to follow the path.

On either side of the path were rows of flowers with heads of quivering flames that bathed the lane in a warm orange glow. Alva called them "Flam" flowers, used to produce the healing Flam Oil he carried in his silver pouch. Kay wondered at their magical beauty, lost in their lulling flames, until a thunderous screech shattered the peace.

Kay and Alva jumped into thorny rose bushes and wormed their way through the branches, scratching their skin, as giant Barbastelle bats flew across the castle gardens. The bats eventually disappeared from view, and Kay and Alva crept out from the thorny bushes, rubbing the scratches on their skin. They shared a nervous glance and braced themselves... they had reached their destination.

Ater Castle was a colossal, haunting building, with glistening surfaces that reflected the white and red of the moons. Many sharp turrets pierced the night sky and created long shadows across the garden where Kay and Alva stood. The windows were thousands of shimmering silver ovals against the black stone walls that reminded Kay of the Onyx Nymphas' white eyes. The castle's double doors were like the Black Gate, with two entangled trees closing the entrance.

Kay and Alva got as close as they dared and then hid themselves amongst some tall, dark conifers. Alva reached into his silver pouch as it appeared and brought out the plants they had gathered upon the mountains.

"It's time to use the Snow Cream," he told Kay.

Kay nodded, pulling the key from her pocket.

"Yes... let's save Rob."

-Chapter 22-
The Wonders of Snow Cream

Kay watched Alva take out the bundles of twigs they had collected on the mountains and brush his thumbs along them. A sparkly substance gathered on his hand, making a cream. As soon as Alva rubbed the cream in, a section of his hand disappeared.

"Whoa!" Kay said. "So, it can turn us invisible?"

"That's right," Alva said, applying some more of the cream on his body. "The Onyx won't be able to see us, but the bats could *smell* us. The cream will eventually dry up though, and then anyone or anything could spot us," Alva figured. "We'll bring the twigs with us just in case we need to re-apply the cream," he added as Kay began to smother the Snow Cream on her face.

As soon as the smooth cream touched Kay's skin, she received a tingly and prickly sensation. She continued to lather herself with the Snow Cream until only her clothes were visible, floating by themselves. Kay covered her clothes in the substance too and then they were ready.

Kay couldn't see Alva at all, so it was difficult to know where he was. She groped around and listened for his voice but couldn't find him.

"Alva," Kay whispered.

"Kay?" Alva replied, sounding just as confused.

Kay eventually found Alva's hand, and she held it tightly so they could stick together. He pulled her towards one of the doors of Ater Castle. The door had a detailed image of mountains etched across it, and Kay noticed a keyhole in its centre, recognising the familiar shape of her Onyx key. Kay removed the key from her pocket and gave a sharp intake of breath as the Onyx eye opened. Kay composed herself and approached the door. The black vine on the key began to glow and flew into the lock by itself, as though magnetised. The key turned sharply and the door creaked open. Kay removed the key from the lock, and she and Alva took their first few steps into the castle.

In front of them was a long bleak corridor, vaguely lit by rows of Loom Stones floating above their heads. The interior was decorated with black stone tiles and dark precious rocks adorned the arched ceiling, like lustrous diamonds. Upon the walls hung great paintings of battles and soldiers with reflective stones embedded in their eyes, their fixed stares glimmering hauntingly in the gloom. The paintings looked ancient, and it seemed that the Onyx Nymphas were proud of their past.

Kay and Alva paced unseen through the castle, the deserted corridors getting gradually darker. The corridors were extremely long and winding, and Kay grasped Alva's hand tighter so they wouldn't be separated. Many of the corridors branched off in different directions, and although Kay couldn't see Alva, she knew he was fretting about which route to take.

"Rob will be in the dungeons," Alva whispered, "so that *should* be below ground level."

Kay made a small agreeing noise to Alva and then they took the darkest tunnel.

As they descended deeper into the bowels of Ater Castle, Kay thought about Rob; they had been separated for too long and reuniting with him was all she wanted. Watching Rob being snatched away from her at the stadium was the worst thing that had ever happened to her. She just *had* to find him.

The corridors seemed to go on forever. They narrowed, then descended and grew even darker. Kay could see nothing and had to rely on her other senses to lead her. She stretched out her hands to feel her way and listened for any noises, but all was silent.

Suddenly, Kay felt her feet miss the ground and she fell with a clatter, tumbling down a few unseen steps.

"Kay, are you all right?" Alva whispered in panic.

Kay felt her knees ache, but she was able to stand up.

"Yeah, I'm all right," she said with a grimace.

"C'mon, let's keep moving," Alva said encouragingly.

As they continued, Kay was much more aware of the small steps leading deeper and deeper into the lower levels. Soon, it felt as though they had been in the castle for hours.

"Alva, we've been wandering around the castle for ages; I think we're lost."

For a moment Kay thought she had lost Alva, but he eventually spoke.

"We don't know our way around here; all we can do is wander the castle's passageways until we find the dungeons," he replied.

Alva sounded irritated and Kay felt disappointed that he couldn't reassure her. She was exhausted and felt as though Rob were slipping away from her again in this unending maze of darkness.

The screams of a bat sent Kay's heart into a frenzy. The noise was coming from nearby and getting closer with every shrill cry. Kay and Alva heard the scratching of its clawed hands on the stone floor.

"It might smell us," Alva gasped.

Kay's heart began to race, and she stood frozen as the giant bat grunted and growled, heading straight for them. The bat sniffed the air and ground and it became excited. Kay got ready to run, but a whirring noise began behind her and she felt a sudden tug around her waist, lifting her into the air. She realised that the whirring was Alva's wings, beating furiously to escape the bat. The bat released an almighty shriek.

"Where are you?" it growled to the walls. Kay felt her heart jump. She looked down and gasped as the bat scrambled up the walls towards them. Alva plunged back down to the floor to avoid the bat's reach, but the beast heard them and lunged off the wall, almost landing on them. Alva cried out in surprise as they dived out of the way, but the bat heard their panic and ran for them, screeching. Alva launched into the air again, hauling Kay down the corridor with the bat giving chase in a frantic crawl, unable to stretch its wings in the narrow passage. The sound of Alva's wings was loud to the bat so it easily tailed them, and Kay felt that she was slowing Alva down.

"Alva, put me down, we'll be faster if we both run!" Kay called.

Alva agreed and descended rapidly. Kay's feet reached the ground sooner than she expected, causing her to stumble before breaking into a run, the beast right behind her. Both Kay and Alva sprinted, holding hands so they wouldn't collide. They ran as fast as their legs would allow, the noise of their feet sounding like bombs echoing in the corridor. The bat eventually fell behind, but Kay and Alva kept on running until they lost the creature completely. After a few bends in the corridors, they slowed to a walk, gasping for air.

"Wow," Alva said, "that was a close one."

"Yeah, but where are we now?" Kay quizzed.

The passageway they were in was much brighter than the others and was superbly decorated with jewel-encrusted statues. Kay noticed most of the statues were dragons with Onyx Nymphas on their backs, heavily armoured, ready for battle.

"Alva, are there dragons in Nymphas' World?" Kay asked, studying the ornaments.

"What gave you that impression?" he said with a chuckle.

Kay gave a smirk, although she knew he couldn't see her.

"The dragons live upon the Onyx Mountains, but they're rarely seen. The dragons that the Onyx ride are Atermons dragons. They're feathered like the Serpenduos, but there are very few of them left now."

"Are dragons really dangerous?" Kay questioned, a little frightened that they could have been attacked by one on the mountains.

"*Wild* dragons are, and if you're an enemy to the owner of a castle dragon then you're likely to be killed in a flash. I suppose it also depends on how old the dragon is or if it's a male or female. Melvin told me that females are always deadlier and harder to train."

"Do they breathe fire?" Kay wondered enthusiastically.

"Yes, if they're old enough. You seem to like dragons. Well, no doubt we'll see them soon," Alva sighed.

"Seriously?" Kay said with surprise.

"Where else did you think the Onyx would keep them?"

he laughed.

Kay went silent and became slightly nervous each time she and Alva turned a corner, in case they came face-to-face with a giant fire-breathing lizard. The ornaments soon disappeared and it became darker again. Each corner they turned led to another, and there were no clues to tell them that they were even going the right way. Kay felt tired and tried to rub her eyes, but this proved difficult when she couldn't see her hands and she ended up poking her eye instead.

"Ouch!" she moaned.

"You okay?" Alva asked.

Kay felt embarrassed about explaining this, so she just replied, "Yeah," and closed the subject and her eye for several moments.

Just when Kay thought they'd be wandering the castle forever, hope appeared. A descending spiral staircase was in sight, with Loom Stones lighting the way. Kay felt both excited and afraid of what was down there.

Kay and Alva took their first steps on the stairs and almost tumbled down them, as they couldn't see where they were putting their invisible feet. Alva kept bumping into Kay, almost toppling her over. He wasn't used to stairs. *Maybe being invisible isn't such a good thing after all*, Kay thought glumly.

Flashes of light suddenly flared up from below and roaring flames could be heard nearby. Kay and Alva tiptoed down the remaining stairs and hid as they spotted two Onyx Nymphas guarding cages of fearsome dragons. They held their breath as one of the guards charged by them to climb the steps. He vanished out of sight and Kay and Alva were left with only one Onyx guard to get by.

"This must be the dragon stables. The dragons can't see us either but have very good hearing, so make sure they don't hear you," Alva fretted.

Kay was first to pass the Onyx guard, stepping as lightly as possible. To her relief, the guard was busy eating and was so preoccupied with his messy meal that Kay slipped by him undetected. She continued on to the bars and felt a sudden wave of heat as thick clouds of smoke billowed out of the bars, making it difficult to see. As Kay fumbled around in the smoke, she could hear an unsettling rumble that rose into a growl, and a shimmering red light scorched the smoke. Kay leapt forwards as a trail of fire blazed across the room, singeing the ends of her hair.

"Let's go," Alva whispered frantically as he brushed by Kay, searching for her hand again.

Kay was panting in panic as Alva pulled her along to the end of the stables where there was another spiral staircase, leading them deeper still.

Kay and Alva hastily descended the stairs onto another level and Kay began to feel even more frightened, for she knew they were now in the right place. Wails and cries emanated from around them and Kay could also hear the sniveling sobs of the prisoners as she passed the rows of cells.

"I'll find the keys, you look for Rob," Alva whispered.

At the very mention of Rob's name Kay sprang into action, on the lookout for her brother. She was worried; although Kay had waited for this moment ever since Rob had been taken, she had no idea what state he'd be in. She continued to scan the cells, hoping she'd spot him soon, because what she saw inside the dungeons distressed her greatly. Kay felt like crying for all the pitiful imprisoned souls, but she kept her faith that her brother would be well enough to travel all the way back home with her.

Kay searched up and down the dungeon until she spotted two Onyx guards patrolling the corridor. She backed against a wall as the guards went by, cruelly laughing and chuckling at all the captives who were wailing in pain. They stopped laughing as they passed by one of the cells, glowering through the bars instead.

"Stupid, dirty Human," snarled one of the guards, rattling the bars threateningly.

Kay threw her hands to her mouth to stop a gasp from escaping. She began breathing heavily with gulping breaths as she waited for the guards to move away. As soon as they were out of sight, she ran over to the cell. It was Rob! He was shivering and dirty but seemed unharmed. He looked miserable and weak, his head hanging limply in defeat.

"Rob!" Kay whispered emotionally.

Rob glanced up, looking confused.

"Kay?" he said in disbelief.

He crawled over to the bars and looked around the seemingly empty corridor.

"Don't worry, Rob, I'm here, we've come to get you out," Kay said to him.

Kay's stomach gave a jolt as her hands reappeared before her.

"No," she murmured, "the Snow Cream's worn off."

"Kay! How did you get here?" Rob questioned excitedly as Kay materialized before him.

"There's no time to explain," Kay answered, panicking.

At that moment, there was a struggle at the end of the dungeon. Alva had been discovered by the two Onyx guards

193

and Kay heard him shout, "Tanglet". The guards were suddenly bound in a thick elastic web and they fell helplessly to the ground. Alva sprinted over to Rob's cell with a bunch of keys jangling in his hand. Alva saw one of the keys glow, and inserted its vine into the cell door. At once the barrier unlocked, opening creakily. The other prisoners began an uproar, pleading for Alva to set *them* free too. Rob staggered out of his cell and Kay grasped him into a longing hug. Alva fumbled with the keys and let out the prisoner next to Rob. The prisoner thanked Alva over and over.

"I trust you to know who's worthy to be freed," Alva said to the prisoner, handing him the keys.

"Thank you," the prisoner said again, accepting the keys.

"Can you walk?" Kay asked Rob.

"Yeah," Rob grimaced, taking a few steps. "We need to get out of here now; I can't go back in there!"

They all ran up the spiral staircase and raced through the dragon stables, with another call of "Tanglet" to wrap up the guard, and back up to the corridors.

"This way!" Rob called out. "I know the way out of here!"

Rob led the way, storming far in front, with Kay close behind him and Alva looking over his shoulder to make sure no one pursued them.

The corridors eventually reached ground level. It was hard to see, but they rushed forwards, eager to escape the castle. Kay felt nervous. They had found Rob, but Kay was worried that they might not be able to find their way out of the castle. She was glad that Rob seemed certain of the way.

"They brought me this way when they took me to the dungeons," Rob explained as they ran. "When they put me in there, I thought I'd never see daylight again," he said sadly.

"They left me there all night and in the morning that *General* brought me out of my cell, forcing me to tell him about *you*," he said to Kay. "He said that he knew there was another Human and he wanted me to tell him where you were, but I wouldn't tell him. He didn't like that," Rob told them with a shiver.

"I'm sorry, Rob. We tried to get here as soon as we could," Kay explained, but Rob smiled.

"Thanks for coming after me, little sis," he croaked with emotion, clasping her hand as they ran, and Kay smiled back at him.

Kay, Alva and Rob ventured up more stairs, and Rob directed them through a maze of tunnels until they saw a set of thick, decorative doors up ahead.

"This way!" he called, until they stood at the entrance to a hall. Kay and Rob squinted through the doors and Kay gasped at the crowded room.

Hundreds of Onyx Nymphas sat comfortably upon rows of fur chairs, feasting upon a hearty meal with the hum of conversation filling the air. The hall had a high arched ceiling and there were occupied chairs climbing the walls all over the oval room.

"We can't go in there!" Kay protested.

"There's no other way," Alva squeaked.

"Well..." Rob whispered, bracing himself as he tiptoed silently into the room.

Kay prayed that no one would notice him slink by. She edged into the room next, her heart slamming against her ribs, but she slipped by undetected. She motioned for Alva to follow, but as he stepped into the hall, one of the Onyx guards glanced his way. It took a few seconds for her to process what she was seeing, whilst Alva stood rigid.

"Alva, run!" Rob called out.

Alva ran and the Onyx Nympha belted out a wail.

"Prisoners escaping!" she cried, and at once, all the Onyx guards in the room flew at Kay, Alva and Rob as they fled the hall.

-Chapter 23-
Ater

The Onyx Nymphas yelled terrifying threats as they stormed down the corridor after them. Kay, Alva and Rob dashed through the passages, but Rob halted abruptly and darted back towards the Onyx guards.

"No!" Kay and Alva wailed, but Rob didn't stop.

As the Onyx guards came charging up to him, Rob latched onto an iron gate that was hinged in an archway. He swung the gate forcefully and it shut with a gong, the sound carrying through the castle.

Rob fell back from the force and the Onyx guards crashed into the barrier, unable to open it or cast spells past it. Rob walked up to the gate and smirked.

"Yeah, let's see you catch us now," he yelled, "you evil blue-faced freaks! I hate you! I hate you all!" Rob screamed with a tremble.

Kay ran up to her brother and tugged him away from the gate.

"Let's get out of here," she said.

They left the Onyx guards trapped behind the gate and ran along the corridor, each clutching their sides from stitches. There were stairs reaching up again and Rob paused.

"This isn't the right way," he said to them. "We must have missed the way out."

"We can't go back," Alva told them hurriedly, "the Onyx will be catching up with us."

"What's that?" Kay quizzed them both, looking up ahead.

Hanging along the far wall of the corridor was a large, colourful object. Kay, Alva and Rob cautiously approached it until they were near enough to see that it was a giant pair of sculpted concrete lips!

"Keep going," Alva whispered to them, as Kay and Rob stopped to stare, but the lips began to shriek.

"Little voices, little voices in my castle!" the lips boomed.

It couldn't see, but apparently it could hear. Kay and Rob jumped back with fright and Alva seemed paralysed.

"Who stands before me?" it cried.

"What are you?" Kay yelled back.

"I?" it yelled. "I am Ater herself!"

"Don't speak to her, Kay," Alva called.

"But what if it can help us get out of the castle?" Kay suggested.

"Kay, it *is* the castle," Alva said.

"Then it can tell us the way out," Rob figured, as he wandered over to the lips. "All right, you, tell us how to get out of here," Rob demanded.

"You'll never get out of here," the lips cackled.

Rob kicked Ater's bottom lip and she gave a squeal.

"How dare you!" she raged.

The whole castle trembled and Kay, Alva and Rob had to balance themselves.

"You tell us or I'll do it again," Rob shouted, and the castle growled.

Rob punched Ater's upper lip repeatedly when, all of a sudden, her lips latched onto his arm. Kay darted over to Rob as he was slurped into Ater's mouth and she clutched onto his leg, but she too was consumed, her upper half now hanging over a bricked throat. Kay stared downwards as she began to slip towards a black void.

Both she and Rob cried out, but as Kay's feet left the ground, something caught hold of her jeans. Alva was trying to haul them out, but the weight of Kay and Rob took the little strength he had left, and he fell down the throat with them.

They all plummeted down a brick chute in pitch darkness. Suddenly, Kay's stomach gave a lurch as she was yanked upwards. She heard a whirring noise and saw that Alva was flying, holding Kay and Rob with all his might. Kay and Rob were swung around as Alva tried frantically to keep them up, but his wings gave way and they all tumbled down the shaft again. They dropped, on and on, until they landed with a painful crash.

*

"Kay, are you all right?"

Kay awoke to Alva's voice, opening her eyes to see him and Rob kneeling around her. She felt throbbing bruises all over her body but no broken bones. She rubbed her head and glanced around; they were still in Ater Castle.

Her heart gave a sudden jolt as sneering blue faces emerged from the shadows behind Rob and Alva.

"Look out!" Kay wailed as a dozen Onyx guards cornered them.

Rob was snatched first and then Kay was painfully hauled off the ground. The Onyx guards were more wary of Alva as he pointed his Virga at them.

"Let my friends go," he demanded.

They all stood silent, scowling at him. Then one lunged at Alva and wrestled the Virga from his hand. Alva was now powerless and dragged over beside Kay and Rob. Kay knew that there was no escaping now.

"Take them to the prince," yelled the Onyx guard with Alva's Virga.

They were dragged away, struggling and screaming. Every bone in Kay's body ached, and her struggles were weak and pitiful. It seemed as though Alva felt the same way, after all they'd been through, but Rob battled on. He couldn't give in; he knew what was in store for them if they failed. He tried to pull away as hard as he could. He even broke free a few times but was immediately caught again by other guards, grabbing a hold of him tighter than before.

Eventually, they reached the upper levels of the castle, climbing up many grand staircases along the way. They entered an opulently decorated room and the Onyx guards flung Kay, Alva and Rob to the hard ground. The guards stood back to reveal a throne at the back of the room, where a Nympha of royalty sat with General Douglas Slate at his side.

"Your majesty, Prince Oswald, these are the intruders within the castle, sire," the Onyx guard with Alva's Virga announced with a bow.

The prince stood up, tall and lean, and looked down upon Kay, Alva and Rob with disgust. He resembled the other Onyx Nymphas in appearance, but his clothes exceeded anything Kay had ever seen. The material was a rich, dark red fur pelt and it dazzled with gems. Jewellery covered any exposed skin and even his pupilless eyes shone like pearls, making his whole appearance sparkle.

"How did they get in the castle?" the prince asked his guards. "Search them!" he bellowed.

Kay, Alva and Rob were searched. From Rob, nothing was found. They took Alva's Virga and belt along with all its accessories. Kay was searched too, and they found the Onyx key.

"Sire, I found this. The Human must have used it to get in the castle," called the Onyx guard holding the key.

Prince Oswald approached Kay and snatched the key from his guard.

"Where did you get this?" he questioned her in frustration.

"Your stupid guards dropped it when they took my brother prisoner," Kay said angrily, and the prince frowned.

"General, dispose of these intruders at once *and* kill the prisoner, we don't want my brother to find out about this."

The prince left the room without a second glance at them, and General Slate stepped forwards. He laughed cruelly and peered down at Kay with haunting white eyes. Rob crawled along the floor next to Kay, and Slate sneered at them both.

He turned his gaze to Alva.

"Ah, yes, I remember you; the Ever who hid them at the stadium."

Alva was trembling in the presence of Slate, and Kay was scared too. Her legs had turned to jelly and her mouth was dry of words as she stared up into Slate's white eyes.

"Did you honestly believe you could just walk in and out of Ater Castle without being caught?" He laughed mockingly as he paced around them.

His hair shimmered in the light as he circled; it was a rich, dark blue and Kay was reminded of a strutting peacock.

Rob stood up bravely.

"Took you a long time to catch us though, didn't it?" Rob said in the cheekiest manner he could muster.

Slate's mouth curled into a more terrible grin.

"I hope you enjoyed your little run around the castle. Your escape attempt has only shortened your life, Human. Was it worth it?" he smirked.

"You're pathetic," Rob remarked boldly.

Slate stopped grinning. "No, your escape attempt was pathetic. Never mind, I suppose this little plan of yours worked to our advantage. Now we have *both* Humans *and* the traitor," he laughed, as he glanced at Kay and Alva.

"You won't get away with this," Alva whimpered. "King Edwin will…"

"You're in Ater," Slate interrupted. "King Edwin can't save you here. Unless… he wants a war," he finished with glee.

Alva rose up from the floor in protest.

"So, that's what you want… a war!" he cried furiously.

Slate smiled, knowing that he'd angered Alva.

"A war is coming, little Ever; it's inevitable and there's no escaping it. Not that it's any of your concern, since you won't live to see it," he sneered.

"You're crazy!" Alva shouted, trembling.

Slate paced back and forth, clearly delighted with Alva's reaction. He then knelt down beside Kay, and she stared into the pupilless eyes of the Onyx Nympha who had turned her days in Nymphas' World from magical to miserable.

"Who are *you*?" he questioned her.

Kay remained silent, feeling defeated. She stared at her reflection upon the dark polished floor. She was dirty, with cuts and bruises across her face.

"Well?" Slate growled, making her jump.

"My name is Kay," she croaked meekly.

"And what are you to this?" he said, indicating Rob with a clawed finger.

"I'm his sister," Kay replied, and Slate's grin widened.

"Leave her alone," Rob barked at him.

Slate grabbed Kay by her hair and pulled her up. Rob was horrified by this. He ran over to Slate and pushed him away from Kay.

"I said leave her alone!" Rob growled.

"You'll pay for that, Human!" Slaye yelled at Rob.

The Onyx guards gathered, ready to attack Rob. "No! I'll do it," Slate commanded.

He pointed a dazzling shard of crystal protruding from his wrist. Rob stood firm, protecting Kay from whatever came their way.

"No, please, stop!" Kay wailed, but Slate ignored her cries.

"Flam!" he yelled, and a sphere of flames blazed through the air towards Rob.

A voice from behind Kay shouted, "Aquati," and gushing water splashed onto the fireball, extinguishing the flames to a puff of smoke. Alva stepped forward with the magical seeds from his silver pouch in hand, ready to fight.

At first Slate was furious, but his gritted teeth relaxed into a grin.

"You want to battle with me, little Ever?"

Alva glared back at Slate, taking another seed in hand.

Slate was amused by this and so he called for one of his guards to bring him "magic rocks".

"This shall be enjoyable," he chuckled, and then he skimmed a sharp black rock along the ground, bouncing towards Alva.

"Sharda!" Slate barked and the rock split, firing needle-sharp shards at Alva that cut into his arms and face.

Alva wiped the blood from his cheeks with a scowl and furiously threw a seed at Slate.

"Tendrila!" Alva screamed, and vines sprang from the magical seed towards Slate, but he was ready.

The General tossed another sharp rock that shredded the vines, followed by several more rocks that showered down upon Alva.

Alva ducked, rolling over to where Kay and Rob were standing. All three of them then had to move as the rock shards whistled through the air. Alva attempted to fire back another seed, but Slate had already conjured a spell; the fight was too easy for him.

"Flam!" cried Slate, and a fireball flew at Alva.

"Ark!" Alva responded, and his seed formed a bark shield that blocked the fireball before shriveling to a crisp.

Alva grasped onto his next seed, but Slate had become bored with their little game. He spread out his wings and a thick mist surrounded him, obscuring him from view.

Alva was confused. There was a silence in the room and everyone, including the Onyx guards, tried to see where Slate had gone.

Then Kay spotted him at the other side of the hall as he hurled a rock at Alva once again.

"Alva, look out!" Kay screamed, but it was too late and Alva was struck down by the shards with a wailing cry of pain.

Alva lay motionless on the stone floor, covered in severe cuts. Kay gasped and ran towards him, fearing the worst.

-Chapter 24-
Kay's Gift

Kay knelt down beside Alva and shook his body, frantically looking for a sign of life, but he didn't stir. Rob ran over beside her just as Alva groaned, opening his eyes.

"Kay?" he croaked, confused about what had happened.

Kay was relieved he was alive but also enraged. Alva was injured badly. The rocks were embedded in his skin and a rather large shard protruded from his forearm. She took the bag of seeds from Alva's hand and rose to meet Slate. Kay didn't know what she was doing, but she had to try and defend the others.

"Kay, no, don't," Rob yelled, but Kay didn't listen.

Slate laughed at her as she stood with the seeds, but Kay didn't care, she wanted to fight him after all he had done to her family and friends.

"A Human that thinks it can perform magic; how entertaining!" he chuckled. "Okay, Human, let's see what you can do before I destroy you, and believe me, this time I'll kill," he told her keenly.

Slate tossed a rock into the air and bellowed his spell excitedly. Kay grasped a seed rapidly as the rock slices sped towards her.

"Ark!" Kay cried, and three bark shields sprouted up to protect her. She hid behind them as the shards fell, and then she rose up from her hiding place and threw a water seed.

"Aquati!" she yelled as Slate cast a ball of fire towards her.

The flames were instantly extinguished, and Slate's face was contorted with rage. He fired two rocks into the air at the same time, confusing Kay.

"Flam!" he cried and then vanished behind grey smoke as two balls of fire roared for Kay.

Kay ducked behind the bark wall, but the first fireball burnt it to ashes. She then dived to avoid the other, but the flames seared her shoulder and she yelped in pain. She quickly stood up to find Slate, but she couldn't see him; smoke had filled the room, hiding the Onyx general.

Her vision was starting to blur, and she could hear Rob calling to her. Kay heard a slight noise behind her and then she was knocked to the floor. Slate rolled Kay over onto her back with one shove of his talon-like foot and pointed his crystal Virga.

"You played well, Human, but you lost!" he chuckled.

Slate was about to kill her but was interrupted by a thunderous blast that echoed through the room.

"Kay?" a voice yelled through the smoke.

Slate was distracted, and Kay quickly scampered away. Slate chased her, vehemently shouting spells. Kay dodged everything that flew at her as she desperately tried to locate the voice. The voice came again. It was squeaky, familiar and closer than she had heard it before.

"I'm over here!" Kay cried.

Suddenly, from the smoke, a Quatmus appeared with an Ever Nympha following behind him.

"Aylwyn!" Kay cried. "Melvin?" she added in surprise.

He looked different without his Ever guard uniform on.

"C'mon Kay, this way," Melvin hollered.

Kay stumbled after them, but another figure jumped out from the smoke — Slate had found them.

"Vanqeath!" he yelled, shooting at Kay. Kay fell backwards, avoiding the deadly spell.

"Bubblo!" Melvin cried out, and Kay found herself encased inside a giant blue bubble.

Aylwyn attacked Slate, biting into the arm that held his Virga, while Melvin rapidly manoeuvred Kay's bubble out of the hall.

"Where are Rob and Alva?" Kay called out desperately, hoping they were safe, but Melvin couldn't hear her.

The corridors were dark so Kay couldn't see a thing. Her heart was beating quicker and quicker and she was trembling from shock. Figures appeared up ahead, and Kay began to panic until she recognised Merlin, without his uniform, accompanying a bubble with Rob inside. Beyond him was Jasmine, soaring beside Alva, who was also in a bubble. Kay glanced behind her and saw Aylwyn running after them.

The castle was in uproar — ornaments were smashed along the corridors where spells had been fired, and screams and shouts reverberated off the walls all around them.

Suddenly there was a wail and a flash of light appeared. Kay's bubble burst and she crashed to the floor, painfully. Kay then saw the outline of a bat racing towards her, but Merlin shot at it before it could strike. The beast dropped limply to the ground, and for a moment everything was quiet. Kay saw that Rob and Alva were no longer in bubbles either, and she was relieved to see that Alva was now standing.

Aylwyn growled as figures approached. These Nymphas were not Onyx though; it was two Ever Nymphas, dressed in rags.

"Don't shoot!" one of them called out as the other Ever Nympha backed away from the advancing Aylwyn.

Before anyone else could speak, a loud bang exploded in the corridor and one of the Ever Nymphas was hit, then the other.

"Run!" Jasmine shouted, and they all dashed through the castle, keeping ahead of the pursuing Onyx guards.

Melvin knew the way and he led his family towards safety.

"How did you get here?" Alva asked Merlin as they ran.

"We captured a bat," Merlin told him in a disapproving tone.

"Yeah, we forced it to let us in the garden and then into the castle," Melvin said menacingly.

"But we left it tied up in one of the pantries," Merlin added with disappointment.

"Snow Cream is also a good trick when you don't want to be seen," Jasmine said, eyeing Alva suspiciously.

Daylight now brightened the corridors and Kay began to realise it was morning. The next moment, light flooded from a door Melvin opened and Kay was met by a cool, fresh breeze; they had found the exit.

Kay, Rob, Alva, Aylwyn, Jasmine, Melvin and Merlin all broke free from Ater Castle's clutches. There was a great cry from the castle walls, and Kay knew it was Ater Castle herself, outraged by their escape.

It was dawn and the sun was beginning to rise. It was magnificent after all the darkness of the castle corridors. Ater

Garden was bathed in daylight, and Kay spotted the Tree of Knowledge in the distance, still shivering in the gloom cast by the bubble around it. It seemed that the tree had a never-ending punishment of being deprived of sunlight, but still the evil lived.

The Flintly Bugs were hovering harmoniously over the garden ponds, and the plants bloomed to catch the first rays of light. Kay could see the path home stretching out across the garden before them, and the sight brought tears of joy to her eyes. She then noticed four Mini-ponies hiding near them in a cluster of trees and Jasmine, Merlin and Melvin rushed over to them, jumping onto their backs. Fulgur and Fidus were there, safe and unharmed. Jasmine mounted Fidus, whilst Melvin and Merlin climbed upon much larger silver ponies. Rob joined Melvin, and Kay and Alva scrambled onto Fulgur's back.

"Hold on tight," Kay heard a gruff voice call.

She looked around to see who had spoken, alarmed that it might be an Onyx guard but then realised that she had heard Fulgur speak.

Without another word they raced onwards through Ater Garden, with Aylwyn at their side, and Kay knew by everyone's expressions that they weren't out of danger yet.

Familiar cries carried through the wind, and Kay looked around and saw bats soaring from the rooftop of Ater Castle. Upon them were Onyx riders, and Kay knew that the Onyx Nymphas had the advantage when they were flying.

Kay held on tightly to Alva, although he was barely strong enough to hold Fulgur's reins himself. She saw Melvin call to Rob, and Rob brought out a silver shield from a leafed pouch attached to their pony's saddle. He then placed the shield at their backs to protect them. On the next pony, Merlin doubled back to his mother with his own shield as the bats approached closer.

"No, give it to Alva and Kay!" Kay heard Jasmine cry, and Merlin tossed the shield over to Kay.

Kay caught it just as something whizzed past her ears, hitting the ground with a small explosion.

"We're in range, split up," Merlin cried.

At that moment more spells flew through the air and the bats swooped down, talons at the ready. The ponies dispersed to avoid the swiping strikes of the bats, but the Onyx guards continued their shooting, sending flaming arrows down upon them. Some hit off the shields and others only missed them by fractions.

Merlin decided it was time to attack back. He pointed his Virga to the skies and shot spells at the Onyx guards. Up ahead was a gathering of tall trees, and all of the ponies dashed in.

"How are we going to get out the gate without a bat to open it?" Merlin shouted frantically.

"There has to be a way," Jasmine yelled in a panic.

"I can get us out the gate," Kay piped up. "I can speak *mammal!*"

The three older Nymphas looked unconvinced.

"She can, Mum, Kay got us in here," Alva confirmed.

"Really?" Jasmine said with surprise.

"That's not possible," Merlin exclaimed, still doubting Kay.

Jasmine looked thoughtfully at Kay and nodded with a small smile.

"She can do it; let's get out of here," Jasmine cried with authority.

The ponies galloped beneath the cover of the trees with the bats still screeching overhead. Kay became extremely nervous, knowing they were all counting on her, but there was no time to think about it as the Black Gate loomed ahead.

Aylwyn caught up with them, gasping, as they neared the Black Gate. The bats went silent, and the Onyx guards positioned them around the clearing between the trees and the gate.

"We're going to have to run through them," Melvin told them all. "Have your Virgas and shields ready."

There was a pause and then Melvin cried, "Now!"

The ponies raced out of the trees towards the gate and Kay readied herself to open it. Arrows fired down upon them, exploding with flashes of light as they hit the shields. The bats dived swiftly, swiping at the ponies and clashing with the shields as Kay, Rob, Aylwyn, Alva and his family fought them off. One swooped towards Kay and Alva, preparing to strike, when it suddenly screamed and dropped out of the air. Kay and Alva gasped as the bat crashed to the ground like a stone, Melvin leaning from his pony with his Virga glowing and a look of relief on his face.

More Onyx riders flew out from the castle roof on their bats, and everyone panicked. The remaining Onyx guards swooped down, shooting more arrows, and Kay screamed for Fulgur to get her close to the gate. The Mini-pony bowed his head and charged forwards, the other ponies closing ranks to cover Kay with their shields. Kay searched within her to cry out like a bat, but what came out wasn't bat-like at all, and the gate remained tightly shut. Kay tried again, but still the gate didn't budge.

"C'mon, Kay!" came shouts of panic from all directions.

It was up to her; if she couldn't get the gate to move, they'd all be dead. Aylwyn ran beside her.

"You did it before Kay, just think of a bat cry," he prompted.

The bats were closing in, and Kay desperately cried out again, screaming as loud as she could. The gate began to move but not quickly enough. One of the bats landed on Merlin, making his pony buckle from underneath. Jasmine hit the bat and its rider with the Tanglet spell, causing them to tumble to the ground in a giant ball of tangled web. Merlin and his pony both leapt to their feet, unharmed, and all of them ran through the now partially open gate.

"Run for the mountains, I have a plan!" Aylwyn called.

"Aylwyn has a plan, follow him," Kay relayed to the others.

"Follow him? Are you mad?" Merlin cried back.

"Just do it!" Kay said, and Alva made Fulgur pursue Aylwyn.

The others continued after them in a desperate attempt to escape the Onyx Nymphas.

-Chapter 25-
Mons Pass

Each pony galloped for the mountains, after Aylwyn. The Quatmus sprinted past the Onyx-Stone staircase that led up Mount Tremors, and Kay had no clue where he was leading them. The Onyx Nymphas loomed overhead, their fire-arrows showering down. Melvin and Merlin did the best they could to protect their family and friends, but the Onyx Nymphas were a strong force by air.

Kay, Alva, Fulgur and Aylwyn stormed ahead, knowing the others would follow. Aylwyn stopped suddenly and began to scratch at the mountainside, like a dog retrieving a bone.

"What are you doing?" Kay called to him frantically.

"What's going on, Kay?" Alva cried to her.

The Quatmus murmured, "Mons," and continued to dig at the mountainside. The mountain stone tore away easily, and Kay was beginning to see that Aylwyn was digging at a covered cave.

"Look, it's hollow. Aylwyn's found a hiding place," Kay gasped.

"It must be the Mons Pass," Alva cried out.

He jumped off Fulgur and began to dig with the Quatmus. Melvin, Rob, Merlin and Jasmine caught up, the arrows now pinging off the mountainside. Aylwyn managed to wriggle into the hollow, followed by Alva. Fulgur reared back on his hind legs as the arrows swished by him, and he stomped his front hooves into the mountainside, which began to crumble. The force from Fulgur's blow knocked an entrance hole into the mountain and all the ponies charged inside with their riders.

"The Mons Pass," Melvin whispered in surprise.

He got off his Mini-pony and ran over to the entrance.

"What are you doing?" Merlin shouted to his brother.

"Everdam!" Melvin called, and his Virga shot an electrical green bubble that covered the entrance. Melvin then whispered a word no other could hear — a password.

"How can you place an Enchanted Concealment on Onyx territory?" Merlin asked, bemused.

"Because this is not Onyx territory," Melvin said.

"You mean we found the Mons Pass? But it's been lost for years!" Jasmine recalled.

"Aylwyn found the passageway," Kay piped up, smiling at the Quatmus.

He smiled back, showing off all his sharp teeth and bowed. Then the Quatmus rose up and he growled as a sound rippled across the bubble's surface; the Onyx guards had arrived.

"Stay where you are, you're all under arrest!" one of them cried out.

"I think you'll find it pretty hard to arrest us now," Melvin laughed, and then he turned to his family, Kay, Rob and Aylwyn. "We should head *this* way," he said sarcastically, ushering them away from the Onyx guards. Some of the Onyx guards tried to break into the bubble, but were unsuccessful and thrust away into the air by the bubble's repelling surface.

The Ever Nymphas laughed and Kay and Rob giggled too as they all turned from the dumbfounded Onyx guards and looked onwards to what lay ahead. The underpass was dark, but from what Kay could see, the tunnel appeared naturally formed, with jagged rocks like icicles dangling from the roof.

Melvin walked up to Rob upon his pony.

"You can stay on my Mini and I'll walk," Melvin told Rob, who looked worn and weak after his days in prison.

Kay wanted to get down from Fulgur and go to Rob, but she felt too tired. She began to hear strange sounds close by.

"Oh, awe, eke, aw, ah, oh."

It was coming from Fulgur.

"Fulgur, are you okay?" she asked, knowing he'd understand her.

"Nothing wrong with me... Oh, awe, eke, aw, ah, oh," he continued again.

Kay mustered the energy to slip off him and found that the pony had an arrow stuck in the bottom of his leg.

"Look, you're hurt. Everyone, Fulgur's hurt!" Kay cried out.

"Oh! Fulgur!" Alva exclaimed as he ran over to his Mini-pony and hugged him around his thick neck. Melvin came over too.

"Nothing's wrong with me," Fulgur began shouting. "Let's just carry on! I'm not going to let a silly old arrow stop me!"

Melvin quickly yanked the arrow out of Fulgur's leg, and the pony shrieked in pain. Fulgur collapsed and stared at his injury, looking dazed.

"See? It isn't so bad," the pony whimpered, looking away quickly.

Melvin poured the healing Flam Oil upon the wound and the liquid began working on the pony's injury. Melvin sent

Fulgur to sleep with a spell and then placed him in a hovering bubble. He shrank Fulgur and the bubble and then handed it to Alva.

"There! Fulgur can sleep now, and he'll feel much better in the morning," Melvin promised Alva, and Alva hugged his brother, putting the bubble in his silver pouch.

They travelled on through the pass and Melvin let Alva and Kay ride with Rob on his larger pony whilst he walked beside his mother. Jasmine seemed tired, so she still sat upon Fidus and Merlin was in front, leading the way home. Aylwyn scurried beside Kay, Alva and Rob, listening to Kay.

"You were great battling with the Ever seeds," Alva whispered to Kay, looking proud.

Kay smiled.

"Yeah, I suppose, but I almost died," Kay told him.

"Both of you were completely awesome!" Rob interrupted.

Kay blushed.

"I don't think Kay or I would have done what we did if you hadn't stood up to Slate first," Alva added.

Kay nodded in agreement, and she could see that Rob's cheeks had also flushed a deep red.

"Don't forget Aylwyn and the others. If they hadn't come, we would *all* be dead!" Kay said, looking to the Quatmus beside them.

Up ahead, Kay could see Jasmine, Melvin and Merlin discussing something. They were mumbling and kept glancing back in their direction.

Kay turned to Aylwyn.

"What made you come back, Aylwyn?"

"Well... I was trying to get back to my family, but I

couldn't stop thinking of your mission," Aylwyn explained, looking at Rob. "Anyway, I was travelling back up Mount Intentus at the time when I saw three Ever Nymphas. They seemed worried about something. I guessed it must have been about you two because the mountains are a dangerous place to travel for Nymphas," Aylwyn said to her. "I decided to try and make contact. It was difficult. I couldn't speak to them, so they thought I was trying to attack. The Nympha over there," he said, pointing to Merlin, "he attacked me, hitting me with spells. I turned very small — it was humiliating! I ran away and thought I'd go home, but I had to wait until I was bigger again. Hours went by and the spell wore off. I was about to journey home, but then I heard lots of screaming and shouting. I ran towards the noise and looked down from the rocks and saw the same group of Ever Nymphas getting attacked by bats. Presuming they might be friends of yours, I joined the fight. With my help, the Ever Nymphas fought off the bats and accepted my help, but I still don't believe they understood *why* I was helping them. I think they know now that I'm a friend of yours," Aylwyn pondered aloud. "But as soon as we get to the swamp, I really need to get home. My partner will be worried and my cubs hungry," he added.

Kay told Alva and Rob Aylwyn's tale, and they both thanked him. Kay then looked ahead and saw a light in the distance. They were near the way out of the pass.

"Kay, can Aylwyn answer us this... why didn't we go *this* way to Ater, instead of a three-day trek over the mountains?" Alva quizzed.

Kay had thought about this too and posed the question to Aylwyn.

"Well..." But as Aylwyn began his explanation, Jasmine

interrupted.

"What you and Kay did was very dangerous; you could have been killed!" Jasmine began, wiping tears from her eyes. "I understand why you did what you did but…" Jasmine started to sob.

Melvin stroked his mother's arm to comfort her, and Merlin rode up upon his pony, looking unhappy.

"Just look at the state you've put mum in," Merlin lectured to Alva.

"Look, if Alva and Kay hadn't tried to save me, I would have been killed," Rob told them all.

"Actually, the negotiations for your release were going just fine at Evertrunk Castle, and we were close to resolving the matter peacefully," he fired back at Rob and then turned to Alva again.

"You had to go and cause trouble, didn't you? Why do you always do the wrong thing all the time? Do you know what this could mean?" Merlin questioned him furiously.

Alva took a gulp and replied, "A war."

Kay felt a surge of rage at the way Merlin was treating Alva.

"Talking to the Onyx wouldn't have worked, they're not going to listen to King Edwin, they hate him," Kay shouted angrily.

Merlin scowled at Kay.

"I think *I* know more about the Onyx than you do," he retorted.

Aylwyn was talking behind Kay, trying to tell her something, but she didn't listen.

"I *had* to save my brother; look what they did to him," Kay cried.

"Yeah, I think I know quite a bit about what the Onyx can do to prisoners, because I *was* one," Rob piped up.

"They could have done a lot worse, believe me!" Merlin yelled.

"Well, I wasn't waiting around to find out what they were going to do to Rob, okay," Kay roared back.

"Please stop, all of you!" Jasmine wailed.

Suddenly Kay heard a horrible groaning noise from above.

"You fools!" muttered Melvin. "You've woken the Moaning Rocks with your bickering," he said, rapidly handing Kay and Rob the Ever Shields as the cave's ceiling started to shift.

Everyone began to panic; the rocks released great gravelly moans as they fell from the top of the tunnel. The Nymphas and Humans were split up by tumbling boulders. The ponies were frantic, running out of sight, whilst Aylwyn was trying to dodge the rocks, leaping and bounding in all directions. The Ever Nymphas used their Virgas to place protective blue bubbles all around them, Alva jumping in with Merlin since his Virga had been taken by the Onyx guards. Kay and Rob ducked under the Ever Shields as the rocks came tumbling down.

They all ran for their lives as the boulders bashed the protective magic and the shields. Merlin, with Alva, fought his way to Kay and Rob and cleared a safe route out in front, with Jasmine at their side and Melvin making sure that they all made it through from behind.

Kay's heart was hammering frantically as she tightly grasped the shield and huddled close to Rob.

"I can see the way out," Merlin shouted over the

deafening noise, and they all charged out of the tunnel as the rocks filled the cave, almost burying them in its midst. Melvin just made it in time as he dodged a boulder spinning out from the cave.

"Well, that was lucky," Melvin said breathlessly.

Aylwyn and the Mini-ponies were already out, bashed and bruised but safe. Aylwyn turned to Kay.

"That's why we didn't take the Mons Pass to reach Ater," he said, panting. "It's too dangerous, but when we were fleeing the Onyx guards in Ater, I felt we had no choice but to take our chances with the rocks."

"Sorry I didn't listen to you, Aylwyn," Kay said to him sadly.

She realised that if she had listened to Aylwyn, she would have known that he had been trying to tell her about the rocks.

Kay gazed around and saw that they were in the swamp again; the sights and smells were no better in the daytime, as the foliage drooped all around and its rotten flesh stung Kay's nostrils. They all began to walk along the muddy path towards home, and saw Verli lurking in the murk of the marsh. Kay was scared, but Aylwyn chased them off until the creatures wormed their way back under the muddy waters.

Kay felt a great sense of relief as they neared the end of the swamp, knowing that Ever village was not far away. She began to reflect upon the past few days; she had seen so much and could now appreciate the wonders of magic, as well as understand its grave dangers, when used for evil.

Kay found herself walking beside Jasmine, on Fidus.

"Jasmine... I'm sorry," Kay said timidly.

For a moment, Kay thought she was going to shout at her or start crying again. She looked tired, but she gave her a small smile.

"I understand why you did what you did. Rob's your brother and you had to get him back," Jasmine said, followed by a weary sigh. "When Alva disappeared, leaving a note saying where you'd both gone, I knew I had to go and find him. I wasn't going to wait on King Edwin finding my son, dead," Jasmine finished, the smile falling from her face.

"Thank you for saving us from the Onyx," Kay said, and Jasmine smiled again.

"You're welcome, Kay," she replied, simply, gazing at her safe family, like a shepherd watching over her sheep.

-Chapter 26-
The Maple Tree

At the end of the swamp, Aylwyn had to leave and get back to his family.

"I'll miss you, Aylwyn," Kay said, embracing him.

"I'll miss you too, but no doubt we'll meet again, someday. Take great care and have a safe journey back to Earth," Aylwyn said, with a small bow of his head.

"Goodbye, Kay," Aylwyn said softly and then scampered off into the swamp.

"Bye!" Kay called after him, and the others waved too as Aylwyn left.

The rest continued out of the swamp, eager to return home. Kay could see the wall of Evertrunk Castle and the Sherba plant that draped over it. Luckily, Merlin led them past the Sherba and into the long grass, his steed ploughing through and making a pathway for the others. Melvin's pony powered in after it, carrying Kay, Alva and Rob. Jasmine was last upon Fidus, the shorter pony trotting to keep up.

"So, will you be returning to the castle?" Jasmine asked her eldest son.

"No," Melvin replied. "The king wants us to meet him at our house — he has something to discuss with us," he said nervously.

Jasmine nodded, unsure of this idea, but had no say in the matter.

"So, what do you think your mum's gonna say when you get back?" Alva said to Kay and Rob.

Kay felt slightly afraid of returning home. She knew her mother would be angry with them. Jasmine's spell on her mother had only lasted a day and they had been away for seven days.

"I don't know. It's been quite a long time now. She's probably got the whole world looking for us," Kay replied in shame. "We should never have come here."

"Remember *why* we did it," Rob told his sister. "It was because of Harron; it's all *his* fault," he reminded her.

"But Rob, what will we say to Mum? Will we tell her the truth?" Kay asked.

"Don't be silly, she won't believe us," Rob claimed.

"Then, what *will* we say?" Kay panicked.

"I think you should tell her the truth, just not the whole truth. Miss out that you met me, and that you were almost killed by the Onyx... Oh, and that you were ever in Nymphas' World," Alva advised.

"That doesn't leave very much for me to tell her," Kay moaned.

"We'll think of something," Rob assured her.

Kay pondered what she would say to her mother the rest of the way to Alva's house. *Maybe she'll be so relieved to see us, she won't ask where we've been*, she thought, with little conviction.

They trekked out of the grass and the village was in plain view, looking splendid in the afternoon sun. They trooped through the centre of the village and many Ever Nymphas came out of their houses, just to watch them go by. They stared at them as though they were a circus act, and Kay felt very unwelcome. She guessed by the many frowning faces and shaking heads that everybody knew what they had done.

Kay spotted the Cumber house amidst the other bubbles. As soon as they neared the house, Merlin murmured the password and entered the electric green bubble on his steed. Kay, Alva and Rob did the same as they entered upon Melvin's pony; Fidus trotted in with Jasmine and then Melvin joined them last.

When the bubble swallowed Kay, she felt the familiar sensation against her skin and then the pleasant, warm air inside.

"Aparta!" Merlin called, causing the ground to open up, and the ponies trotted down to their underground stables to rest.

Everyone else clambered through the foxglove petals and slid down the chute. As Kay slid down, she immediately felt a huge sense of relief; Rob was safe. She had done what she set out to do. They all entered the living room and collapsed onto the floating petals.

Tansy bounded through to greet them, pleased that they were back, and Dandy followed in after her. He gave Jasmine and Alva hugs and nodded to Melvin and Merlin, who nodded in return. He smiled to Kay and Rob and then said his goodbyes to all as he left.

Kay wanted more than anything just to go home now, but she was far too exhausted. They all rested a while on the levitating petals until an assertive voice announced, "I'm here," through Melvin's Tactus.

Melvin and Merlin both sprang up and went towards the front door of their house. Jasmine also arose as King Edwin marched into the living room, his wrinkled face looking angry. A majestic robe trailed after him, and his crown sat proudly upon his yellow-grey hair as he looked to Rob, then to Kay and, last of all, to Alva.

"You've probably already heard this, but *that* was a very dangerous thing to do and could now have very serious consequences," King Edwin said gruffly, like a disappointed grandfather.

Kay wanted to tell him that she didn't care what he thought, but she was too exhausted for an argument. Alva and Rob didn't look pleased either, but they remained silent.

"However, I'm glad you all made it back alive," the king added, then he looked at Kay. "I'd like to speak with you, Kay," he began. "I'll be in the kitchen; come alone."

Kay was confused by this but followed the king as commanded.

The king glanced around the kitchen before turning towards her. He seemed very restless.

"Rescuing your brother was very brave, but it's caused a lot of difficulties. It could mean..."

"War," Kay interrupted, her heart feeling heavy.

She had never wanted to cause trouble, but she'd never regret going after Rob.

"Maybe the Onyx *won't* start a war," Kay said hopefully. "I mean, was it *that* big a deal?"

"The Onyx have been looking for an excuse to start a war for decades, and I fear you've just given them one," the king said gravely.

"I'm sorry," Kay piped, "but I *had* to get Rob back."

"I'm glad you got your brother back," he said with a sigh and gave Kay a small smile. "I doubt they would have let him go anyway. The Onyx despise me, and it would have delighted them to kill a Human and slight me at the same time," King Edwin told her.

Kay felt pleased that the king understood.

"Thank you, Your Majesty, but why are you telling me this?" Kay questioned.

"Well, when Nymphas fight, much destruction is caused, and for Humans to be in Edenland in those times; well, it would be very dangerous for them. I suppose what I'm trying to say is that you should never, ever come back here. I think that will be best for all of us," King Edwin suggested, and Kay felt saddened by the thought.

The king seemed sorrowful too, but what he'd said was true. The Ever Nymphas might be in more trouble with the Onyx Nymphas if Kay or Rob were to return.

"I never wanted to cause any trouble for you," Kay said.

"Just promise me that you will not return?" the king asked, and Kay nodded submissively.

"I promise," she uttered.

The king nodded and then he gracefully left the kitchen. Kay followed him out and they met Melvin and Merlin in the hall.

"Kay, Rob, I think it's about time we got you both home," King Edwin announced, and Melvin and Merlin stood to attention.

"Melvin, Merlin, you can both accompany me with the rest of the guard," King Edwin said to the brothers.

"Can I come too?" Alva piped up.

King Edwin looked to Jasmine, and she nodded her consent. Jasmine ruffled Rob's hair, like Kay's mother always did and grasped him into a hug. Rob seemed a little uncomfortable with this but didn't protest.

"Well, goodbye, Rob," Jasmine said and let go, turning to Kay.

She pulled Kay close and gave her an affectionate cuddle as well.

"Goodbye, Kay, dear," she sniffled.

"Goodbye, Jasmine, I'll miss you," Kay said sadly.

She pulled away from Jasmine's embrace and then walked beside her brother as they set out of the house. They passed through the bubble and stepped out into the cold, clean air. Outside, many Ever guards patrolled the area, all the way through the village towards the wood, where the Portal was. Kay trekked beside Alva and Rob with the king leading the way. As they approached Elna Wood, Kay saw the Great Statues. They travelled past the statue of King Edwin himself and there was a great likeness in it. They passed by the other statues, including the Mother of All. She looked exactly as she did in the *Book of All*. Each moved as they had done before, but as they passed the Mother of All, Kay noticed that instead of beckoning them to Edenland like she had done before, she waved them goodbye.

The shrubbery and trees thickened and then Kay saw it: the Portal, bright and swirling.

"Can I go through the Portal with them, just to say goodbye properly?" Alva asked his brothers.

Melvin looked to the king, who gave a stern nod and said, "Be quick."

Alva gave a gleeful smile as he joined Kay and Rob at the Portal. The Humans called farewell to all who had come to witness their departure and took their first step back into the Portal. Alva led the way through the forceful winds and the silence that made Kay feel deaf. Suddenly, Alva's body disappeared into a golden light that also consumed Kay and Rob as they followed behind him.

They all found themselves in the roots of the old Rowan Tree, the familiar earthy smell prevalent in the darkness. Alva walked beside them at first, but as soon as he began to shrink small enough, he flew again, his Nympha Dust sparkling in the gloom behind him. He guided Kay and Rob to the tree's entrance, bringing them back to Earth.

Kay and Rob crawled through the hole in the tree and Alva flew out; he had become the size of a finger again. Kay looked around at Callendar Park Woods. It was so *normal* and *boring* compared to the bright, lush scenery of Nymphas' World. The sun shone through the Rowan Tree's branches and the birds' calls were the usual noises she had heard all her life.

"Well, I guess this is it," Alva said in a squeaky voice.

A lump began to swell in Kay's throat as she thought about saying goodbye to her best friend.

"Here, I want you to have this," Alva said to Kay, placing a tiny object in her hand.

"Growig!" Alva called, and the item began to grow until it was large enough for her to see what it was.

"Your Tactus," she gasped.

"Yeah, so we can keep in contact," Alva replied. "Don't worry, I've got another one."

Kay smiled and placed the ring upon her finger.

They all stared at each other, knowing the time had come.

"Thanks for helping me find Rob," Kay said to Alva.

"Yeah, I owe you one," Rob said to the little Nympha.

Alva grinned.

"That's what friends are for," he replied to them both. "I better get back to my family. If I don't, they might come after me again," he chuckled.

"Yeah, we better get home to our mum too," Rob insisted.

"Well, bye. I'll come and visit some time," Alva said.

"Bye!" Kay said back to him, and Alva flew into the hole in the Rowan Tree and disappeared out of sight.

Kay and Rob both glanced at each other excitedly; they were going home to their mother now. Rob grinned and then raced forth, bounding through the trees. Kay ran after him and in just a few short minutes the main road came into view. They both crossed the road and sped home as fast as they could. They arrived at their street and spotted their house; Kay was terrified about what her mother was going to say, but she was so glad to be home. They ran up the garden, through the door and bounded up the stairs, calling to their mother breathlessly. She responded at once.

"Rob, Kay!" she screamed.

Kay found herself in the familiar hallway of her home, and her mother stood at the living room doorway, paralysed by what she was seeing. Suddenly she darted over to them, screaming their names at the top of her lungs. She yanked them both into a rib-crushing embrace and sobbed noisily, her tears soaking into Kay's hair.

Their mother stood back after several moments, ceased her weeping and just stared at them, looking drained but ecstatic to see them. Fresh tears sprang from her eyes; she was in shock.

This continued for a period of time, but Kay knew the question would come and she was unprepared as to how she'd answer her mother.

"Thank Heaven you're safe," she cried out. "Where have you both been?"

Kay stared at the Tactus upon her finger.

"Well?" her mother demanded.

"Well…" Kay began, "When you let me and Rob go for chips, we saw Harron."

"Who's Harron?" their mother questioned.

"He's a boy in my class, he was gonna do us in, so…" Rob began to explain.

"Someone was going to hurt you?" Belle interrupted with worry and Rob nodded, glancing at Kay.

"And then Alva helped us," Kay added, but her mother had become puzzled.

"Who's Alva?"

"He's a Nympha," Kay said quietly, but her mother still heard.

"What's a Nyma?" she quizzed.

"Kay means a *fairy*, Mum," Rob piped up, but their mother looked completely confused.

"You're trying to tell me you ran away because of *fairies*?" Belle said, raising her voice.

"No, we were trying to hide from Harron, the bully," Rob corrected her.

"For an entire week?" Belle squealed.

Rob went quiet and glanced back at Kay. Kay didn't know what to say, but she could only try and explain.

"The *fairy*…"

"No, don't talk to me about fairies; tell me where you've

both been. I've had the police and everyone out looking for you," Belle said, her eyes welling up again.

"It's true, Mum, we met a fairy and it took us to a different world!" Rob yelled back.

"What are you talking about?" Belle said, quite aggravated now.

"The fairy, Alva, he took us to this place where we could hide from Harron. We stayed there, waiting for him to go away, but then these other Nymphas, I mean fairies, they kidnapped me, and Kay had to rescue me before they killed me."

"Someone was going to kill you?" she asked tearfully, and Rob nodded.

Belle clasped her hand to her mouth and couldn't speak as she took this news in.

"Can you remember anything? What the criminals looked like? What they did?" She asked.

Rob looked at Kay. Their mother wasn't going to acknowledge anything about the Nymphas. Rob gave up and shook his head in reply. Then Belle looked to Kay. Kay felt disheartened but not surprised. She shook her head along with her brother.

Their mother phoned the police, and Kay and Rob gave the officers their story when they came to the house. They both decided to tell the police the truth about the Nymphas, which the police didn't believe and wrote down that they were "suffering from psychological trauma".

"Sometimes kids can make things up when they go through something traumatic. They're scared to tell us what really happened or they block it from their minds. We'll come back tomorrow, Miss. Maybe they'll tell us after they've had a bit of rest," one of the officers told their mother as he left the house.

Belle continued hugging her children long into the evening. Kay and Rob were given a hearty meal and they ate until they could eat no more.

Although Belle couldn't understand what had happened to her children, she was still glad that they were home. She tucked them into their beds and kissed them goodnight. It took quite a while for Kay to fall asleep though. All she could think about was Nymphas' World. Kay stared at the Tactus upon her finger, as a reminder, knowing that it hadn't all been a dream. She peered into the ring's orange stone.

"Alva," she whispered.

The Tactus twinkled and a face appeared. It was Alva.

"Kay, is that you?" he whispered back.

"Yeah," Kay replied. "How're things in Nymphas' World?"

"Well, the Onyx are mad. They're searching all over for you and Rob. Some of the Evers are quite scared, but the Onyx aren't allowed to check our houses. My mum says we're not allowed outside because they might recognise us, so I won't be visiting Earth for a while. How did your mum react?" Alva asked with concern.

"She was quite upset, and I don't think she believes us," Kay said to him.

"You told her about Nymphas' World? Bad idea," Alva commented.

"I didn't want to lie to her, but I suppose she thinks I'm lying anyway," Kay sighed.

Alva looked sad.

"Don't worry, Kay, I'm sure things will go back to normal soon," he assured her.

They said their goodbyes to one another and then the Tactus shimmered back to a glistening orange stone.

Kay stared at the stone a few moments longer and then turned the other way in her bed. It seemed so long ago since she had slept in it last. It was warm and cosy and her bed covers were soft. Kay still thought about Nymphas' World but hearing Alva's voice had given her comfort. She closed her eyes and fell asleep.

*

The next few days saw things gradually return to normal. The police came around a couple more times to see if they had a different story to tell them, but when Kay and Rob continued to talk about the fairies, the police gave up. Belle argued with the police, but they decided it was best not to come back until Kay and Rob remembered what had happened.

Belle had also decided that she would phone Kay's school and the high school Rob would be attending after the summer when Rob informed her that Harron would be at the same school. She didn't know exactly what had happened, but she was determined to put an end to the bullying and set things to rights. Kay doubted that Harron and Margaret would leave them alone, though she hoped that their experiences of Alva's magic might deter them at least for a little while.

Kay spent most of her summer days in her back garden, enjoying the sunshine. She laid out her tartan blanket and sipped lemonade as she watched the birds fly above her in the clear blue sky.

"Out for a picnic again, are we?"

Kay jumped when she heard the voice and turned to see who was speaking to her. It was the garden maple tree. The tree smiled and shook all its red leaves with a giggle. Kay smiled back. She missed Alva, but she was happy she had brought a part of Nymphas' World's magic back with her. Kay could now talk to trees, who were delightful company, and Rob spent more time with her now too. She spoke to Alva every day on her Tactus, and she also found that she had a whole host of other new friends to spend time with. Outside, Kay heard all the mammals talking. Every dog bark was a hello and each meow a good evening. Kay had even befriended a squirrel that had been crossing her garden one day. She'd had many adventures over the summer, going off into Callendar Park Woods, exploring with her newfound friends. Kay now had a craving to discover new places and she didn't need Rob to hold her hand any more. She could handle things by herself and look danger in the eye. It just wasn't the same as Nymphas' World though.

Now that she had her magical gift, she would never be lonely again. She'd always have someone to talk to, but she knew now that she was very different from those whom she associated with on Earth. *I'll go back to Nymphas' World one day*, Kay promised herself.